K

Cruise Ship Christian Cozy Mysteries Series

Book 7

Hope Callaghan

hopecallaghan.com

Copyright © 2016

All rights reserved.

Visit my website for new releases and special offers: hopecallaghan.com

i

Thank you, Peggy H., Jean P., Cindi G., Wanda D. and
Barbara W. for taking the time to preview *Killer Karaoke*,
for the extra sets of eyes and for catching all my mistakes.

A special thanks to my reader review team: Alice,
Amary, Barbara, Becky, Becky B, Brinda, Cassie, Christina,
Cyndi, Debbie, Denota, Devan, Francine, Grace, Jan, Jo-
Ann, Joeline, Joyce, Jean K., Jean M., Kathy, Lynne,
Megan, Melda, Kat, Linda, Lynne, Pat, Patsy, Renate,
Rita, Rita P, Shelba, Tamara and Vicki

Like Free Books?

Get Free & Discounted Books, Giveaways & New Releases When You Subscribe To My Free Cozy Mysteries Newsletter!

hopecallaghan.com/newsletter

TABLE OF CONTENTS

"Be joyful in hope, patient in affliction, faithful in prayer." **Romans 12: 12. (NIV)**

Chapter 1

Annette Delacroix stood on the dock and gazed at the gangway. She lifted the bullhorn to her mouth. "You can do it, Cat," she encouraged.

Millie Sanders, who was standing behind Cat, placed the palm of her hand in the center of Cat Wellington's back and gave her friend a small nudge forward. "C'mon Cat. You're almost there. All you have to do is take a few more steps."

Cat inched her foot forward and quickly pulled it back as she began trembling violently. "Millie, I can't." Her eyes darted fearfully to the dock and the crew who stood nearby, offering moral support.

Cat abruptly shifted to the side, elbowed Millie out of the way and bolted up the stairs before disappearing from sight.

Annette lowered the bullhorn and trudged up the gangway to join Millie. She stared at the empty staircase, and pinched her thumb and index finger a smidgen apart. "She was this close."

"Now what?" Millie asked. "It's been months now since Cat has stepped foot off the ship."

Cat Wellington's fears were understandable. The poor Siren of the Seas employee had suffered unimaginable pain and trauma at the hands of her ex-husband, who was in prison for attempted murder...Cat's attempted murder.

It was apparent after today's exercise Cat needed professional help. Technically, it was none of Millie's business, but she had already approached Doctor Gundervan, the Siren of the Seas ship's doctor, not to mention Donovan Sweeney, the ship's purser who was also Cat's boss, as well as Captain Armati, the ship's captain.

Millie had told them that Annette and she had planned one final intervention, along with several of the crewmembers who were close to Cat, to try to get her to step foot off the ship. It was their last ditch effort and it had failed miserably.

"I guess we move forward with Plan B," Annette said as she shook her head.

"I'll make the call while we're still in port," Millie said. "I was afraid this was going to happen so I brought my cell phone with me." She had tracked down a psychologist on the island of St. Thomas, which was the ship's next port stop. According to the online ad Millie had found, the doctor made "house calls." She hoped the doctor would also make "ship calls."

She placed her backpack on the floor and unzipped the front, pulling out her cell phone and a piece of paper she'd jotted the doctor's number on.

The line rang several times before a recorded message stated that Doctor Rebecca Johansen was with a patient and she would return phone calls in her free time.

Millie left a brief message, pressed the end button and dropped the phone back inside her backpack. "I hope she calls before the ship sets sail so I can confirm an appointment."

"Me too." Annette, head of the ship's food and beverage department, glanced at her watch. "I better get back to the galley."

It was almost time for the lunch crowd to invade the lido deck, which was where the buffet and outdoor grill were located. The crowds would be light since the ship was docked on the small island of St. Croix and many of the passengers had disembarked for a day of sun, sand and solid ground.

The ship had hit some rough weather after departing San Juan, and a minor tropical storm had caused the ship to rock and roll. Millie was used to the rocking and rolling and barely even noticed anymore, except when the crew placed barf bags near the stairwells and elevators.

Millie hurried to deck five, the promenade, to track down Andy Walker, the ship's cruise director. Andy was also Millie's boss.

Millie heard Andy before she saw him. His loud, booming voice echoed in the soaring atrium. "I must have a small stage, a rear curtain and the karaoke equipment set up right here before the ship sets sail at six o'clock."

Andy wasn't yelling, but Millie could tell from the tone of his voice that he wasn't a happy sailor. He was talking in his clipped, no nonsense tone as he faced one of the higher ups in maintenance, judging by the uniform the man was wearing.

"We will move the equipment when we have time. My men are working on the davits," the man calmly informed Andy. "I have a job to do and that's ensuring the safety of both the crew and passengers. Your...project is not a priority."

Millie slowed her pace when she caught a glimpse of the expression on Andy's face.

"That *project* as you call it is my job." Andy's voice raised an octave, and crew and passengers began to take notice of the heated exchange.

"I'm sure Mr..." Millie glanced at the man's nametag. "Mr. Falco will start working on it as soon as possible."

"I will get to it when time permits," the man replied before he turned on his heel and strode out of the atrium.

"I ought to have him fired." Andy shook his head. "You'd think I was asking for the crew to rearrange the entire electrical systems on board the ship instead of moving a small amount of equipment to set up our new karaoke area."

Andy and Millie, along with Danielle Kneldon, who also worked in the entertainment department, had come up with a brilliant plan to move the karaoke venue from one of the smaller, secluded lounges to the main area of the ship in hopes of sparking some renewed interest.

The number of passengers participating in karaoke had been dwindling the last few months and the trio had decided a more central location, with an added twist, would give it the boost it needed.

Millie thought it was a wonderful idea, but it appeared execution of the plan was going to be a challenge.

"Will you be ready to host if Falco can get the equipment in place?" Andy asked.

"Of course," Millie nodded. "I'll check back in a couple hours to see if they're working on it yet. In the meantime, I'll make my rounds."

"Sounds good." Andy lifted his hand in a small salute and headed across the room to chat with the guest services staff. Millie wondered if he planned to stop by Donovan Sweeney's office to discuss Luigi Falco. Donovan's office was directly behind guest services.

The afternoon flew by and Millie checked her phone periodically to see if Doctor Johansen had returned the call. Soon, the ship would set sail and Millie would no longer have cell service.

She left a second, more urgent message, explaining to the psychologist she worked on board a cruise ship that would be docking in St. Thomas in two days and she had a friend who desperately needed help.

Millie hung up, praying the doctor would take the call seriously. For now, all she could do was hope that the doctor would be able to fit Cat into her schedule.

After placing the call, Millie headed back down to the atrium / piano bar area to see if the crew had begun working on the karaoke stage. She was relieved to see four crewmembers assembling the stage and wandered over to check on their progress.

"...by the breaker box right near the theater. He never stood a chance. Electrocution would be my guess."

The words "theater" and electrocution" caught her attention and her first thought was something had happened to Andy. "Is he okay?" Millie asked.

The two men who had been talking exchanged an uneasy glance. "No, he's not. He's dead."

Chapter 2

Millie's heart skipped a beat and the room began to spin. "Andy is dead?"

One of the workers cast a puzzled glance at her. "Who is Andy?"

"Andy Walker, the Cruise Director," Millie said.

"No. We were talking about Luigi Falco, one of Siren of the Seas head engineers." The man lowered his voice. "The last time I talked to him, he was headed to the ship's theater to take a look at a breaker box that was malfunctioning."

"Oh my gosh!" Millie's hand flew to her mouth. "Luigi Falco." She knew exactly who Luigi Falco was. He was the man Andy had been arguing with hours earlier in that exact same spot.

"What a terrible tragedy." Millie turned to go and then turned back as she remembered the reason she was there. "Will the stage and equipment be ready for tonight's first round of karaoke? It starts at 9:00 p.m."

"Yes ma'am." The worker glanced at Millie's nametag. "Miss Millie. We will finish assembling the stage shortly. After that, we'll hook up the electrical and then run some sound checks." He glanced at his watch. "We should be out of here by 5:30."

Millie thanked them for their time and then hurried out of the atrium. She picked up the pace and power-walked to the other end of the ship, to the theater.

Caution tape blocked the entrance to the theater so Millie retraced her steps and headed to a second entrance on the other side of the ship. She slipped inside the dark theater.

Loud voices echoed from behind the stage where the ship's dancers and performers' dressing rooms, as well as the make-up areas and Andy's small office were located.

The voices grew louder as she hurried up the side steps and across the stage.

When she reached Andy's office, Millie could see Andy, front and center. Dave Patterson, Head of Security, Oscar, Patterson's right-hand man, Captain Armati, Donovan Sweeney and two uniformed officers, surrounded him. Judging by the men's uniforms, they were not the ship's officers.

The conversation ceased as Millie approached. Dave Patterson waved her into the room. "I was getting ready to radio you. I'm sure you heard about the unfortunate accident."

Millie nodded her head. "I just heard the news."

"You were one of the last people who spoke with Mr. Falco before his death and we would like you to tell us what you remember about the conversation," Captain Armati told Millie.

Millie sucked in a breath. "Yes, I first met Mr. Falco shortly before his...untimely demise. He was in the atrium, talking with Andy, Mr. Walker."

One of the uniformed men clicked the end of his pen and began jotting notes in a notepad he was holding. "Witnesses report Mr. Walker and Mr. Falco were arguing. Do you recall the conversation?"

Millie gave Andy a quick glance. "I..." Millie's voice trailed off. She knew her answer could incriminate Andy. "They were discussing a project and not completely seeing eye to eye," she said and then quickly continued. "But they were finally able to reach an agreement and Mr. Falco left."

"What happened after that?" the man prompted.

"I watched Andy, Mr. Walker, make his way to the guest services desk. I made my rounds, checking on passengers and the ship's scheduled activities."

"So you never talked to Mr. Falco or Mr. Walker after the incident?"

"It wasn't an incident," Millie said. "It was a boisterous conversation."

The officer glanced at Millie's nametag. "Thank you Ms. Sanders." The comment was Millie's dismissal and she gazed helplessly at Andy and then Captain Armati, who gave her a small nod. She backed out of the room and then headed across the stage. They thought Andy was responsible for the man's murder!

Millie exited the theater and began pacing the outer hall as she mentally replayed what she'd told the authorities. She hadn't intended to throw Andy under the bus and she hoped she hadn't, but the two men had been having a heated discussion.

Had something transpired after Millie departed, causing officials and authorities to suspect Andy's involvement?

She cast a nervous glance in the direction of the theater before heading to the galley to talk to Annette. She was halfway there when she ran into Danielle.

"I've been looking for you." Danielle grabbed Millie's arm and dragged her off to the side, near the stairwell. "I heard Andy is being questioned about a crewmember's death on board the ship. Can you believe it?"

Millie shook her head. "No. I have no idea how the man died, but I would bet my life Andy had nothing to do with it."

Danielle leaned in and lowered her voice. "Rumor is spreading like wildfire that Andy and this Luigi dude were arguing. A short time later, the guy is deader than a doornail and his body found right outside the theater to boot."

"Andy is innocent," Millie insisted. "The authorities can't seriously consider blaming Andy for the man's death. Andy and Luigi Falco had a simple disagreement. People don't kill other people because of a small argument."

Several of the ship's passengers descended the steps, and Danielle waited until they were out of earshot. "No, but I talked to Nikki Tan down in guest services and she said she heard that Andy filed a complaint earlier, insisting the man be fired."

"Does Andy outrank an electrical engineer?" Millie asked.

Danielle shrugged. "Does it matter? The guy is dead and Andy is on the hook."

Muffled steps approached and several new crewmembers wandered down the steps.

After they disappeared from sight, Danielle let out a wolf whistle. "Did you see the tall one with the dark hair? He's a hottie. I need to find out where he works." Danielle didn't wait for an answer as she followed the crew.

Millie shook her head and continued her climb to deck seven, passing by Ocean Treasures, the ship's gift shop where Cat worked. Although the shop was closed while the ship was in port, she caught a glimpse of Cat's signature beehive hairdo as she bent over a display case, rearranging items on one of the shelves in the back.

She slowed, contemplating a quick chat with Cat, but decided to stop by on the way back through, after she talked to Annette.

The galley was a flurry of activity as the crew prepared for the evening's formal night and dinner. It was the cruise ship's gala dining event and required all hands on deck as Annette and her crew worked hard to execute a meal fit for a king, or in this case, paying passengers.

She spied Annette, along with Annette's right hand man, Amit, standing near the dessert prep area.

Millie zigzagged around the gleaming stainless steel counters as she made her way to the other side of the room.

"This is too firm." Annette pressed on the top of the chocolate dish, lightly dusted with powdered sugar. "See? It needs to be a little softer. I should be able to dig into the center and scoop out a spoonful of warm, melted chocolate."

"I'd eat it," Millie quipped as she listened to the exchange. She winked at Amit and he smiled broadly. "Hello Miss Millie. Are you here for a lesson on creating Annette's famous melted chocolate cake?" he asked.

Millie lifted both hands. "No way, but I volunteer to be an official taste tester," she teased.

Annette patted Amit's back. "Keep working on it, Amit. You're getting close." She turned her attention to Millie. "I can guess why you're here." Annette waved Millie to the other side of the galley. "Let's chat in my office."

Annette's "office" was the walk-in dry goods pantry. She led the way across the massive galley kitchen, opened the pantry door and flipped the light on. The women stepped inside. "Andy is on the hook for loathsome Luigi's untimely death."

"Loathsome Luigi?" Millie asked.

"Yep." Annette nodded. "He has...had a reputation for being a real jerk."

"I had no idea. How come I've never heard his name before?" Millie asked.

"We run in different circles, you and I," Annette said. "Plus, I have hundreds of spies running around this ship." She nodded her head toward the room full of kitchen staff.

Millie shifted her gaze to the army of workers darting back and forth inside the kitchen. "True." Her shoulders sagged. "I hope the investigators are able to figure out what happened to Mr. Falco."

A light tap on the outer doorframe interrupted their conversation. "Miss Annette?"

Annette made her way to the exit and Millie followed behind. It was Amit. He glanced from Annette to Millie. "Miss Millie. Suri just come back from his break. He say he pass Mr. Patterson and Mr. Walker on deck two. They were walking toward the jail and Mr. Walker was wearing handcuffs."

Chapter 3

"They arrested Andy?" Millie blinked rapidly as she tried to digest the tidbit of information. "But Andy didn't kill Falco." She shifted her gaze to her friend. "We have to do something."

Annette rubbed her chin thoughtfully. "This is terrible news and you're right." She glanced at her watch. "Unfortunately, it's crunch time for dinner so we'll have to wait until later. Meet me back here around 8:30."

"I – I have karaoke at 9:00 and if Andy is locked up, I'll have to cover for him." Millie continued. "I'll try to swing back by around eleven, if you're still here. The main shows will be over, the dance clubs will have opened up and I'll have more free time."

Annette patted Millie's arm. "Don't worry, Millie. We'll get to the bottom of this."

"I hope so." Millie stepped out of the galley and made her way to the gift shop to chat with Cat, but Doctor Gundervan was inside and they appeared to be having a serious conversation so Millie kept moving. She was on the fence about warning Cat that she'd contacted a female psychologist to meet with her in St. Thomas.

She would still need to get clearance from Captain Armati to allow Dr. Johansen to board the cruise ship so she could meet with Cat.

Captain Armati had invited Andy and Millie to join him at the Captain's Table for dinner, along with some of the VIP passengers, but those plans may have changed now that Andy was locked up.

The captain and Millie had been dating for several months now, although dating seemed like an odd word to use since they couldn't actually "date." There was nowhere to go, other than dine in the captain's quarters.

On rare occasions, when they both had free time and the ship was in port, the captain and Millie ventured off to explore the islands.

Captain Armati...Nic...had mentioned taking Millie snorkeling while they were in St. Thomas but that might not work now that Annette and she had planned an intervention for Cat, not to mention the fact Andy was in the slammer.

Millie frowned at the thought. She needed to track down Dave Patterson to see what on earth was going on, but first she had a job to do, and that was to head down to deck five to greet passengers who were returning from their day on the island of St. Croix.

Danielle was already there, chatting with the young man she'd been chasing after earlier. She turned when Millie approached. "Lorenzo, this is my cabin mate, Millie Sanders. Millie is also Siren of the Seas Assistant Cruise Director."

Millie shook the young man's hand as she studied his face. He was attractive, with olive colored skin, dark, brooding eyes and jet-black hair. "Slick" was the first word that popped into Millie's head.

Lorenzo lifted Millie's hand and kissed the top. "Millee." Her name rolled off his tongue. He gave her hand a small squeeze before releasing it.

"Ah, there are so many beautiful women on board this ship," he murmured.

Millie cleared her throat. "Lorenzo. You must be new. I've never seen you around ship."

"Yes, I uh, just transferred from Marquise of the Seas." Marquise of the Seas was one of Majestic Cruise Lines' older ships. It sailed shorter cruises, mainly to the Bahamas and the cruise line's private island, South Seas Cay.

"I see," Millie nodded. "What department do you work in?"

Lorenzo gave Danielle, who gazed at the man like a love struck teenager, a quick look.

"Housekeeping for now, but I've already put in a request to transfer to bar service."

The conversation ended as a small group of passengers descended on them and Lorenzo excused himself.

After directing the passengers to the lido deck and the grill area, Danielle turned to Millie. "I heard they took Andy down to the holding area," she whispered. "That means they think he had something to do with the crewmember's death."

"I don't believe it," Millie said. "There's no way Andy killed that guy. I don't care what they suspect."

She wondered what evidence they had uncovered, but didn't have time to dwell on it as another group of passengers made their way over.

Millie caught a glimpse of the uniformed officer who had questioned her in Andy's office. He and the other officer disembarked the ship

25

and she was relieved to see that a handcuffed Andy wasn't with them.

After the last passenger had boarded, the crew removed the gangway and shut the outer door. Millie made a beeline for Dave Patterson's office while Danielle headed upstairs to check on the sail away party.

The lights were on in Patterson's office and she could hear the faint murmur of voices on the other side.

Millie tapped lightly on the door and when she heard a muffled reply, she turned the handle and opened the door.

Inside the room were Dave Patterson and Oscar, as well as Donovan Sweeney. Captain Armati wasn't there, but Antonio Vitale, the ship's staff captain, was.

"Come in, Millie." Patterson waved her into the office. "Please close the door behind you."

Millie quietly eased the door shut and stood next to Oscar. "Rumor has it you arrested Andy and he's down here in one of the holding cells."

"He is." Patterson leaned forward in his chair. "We told the St. Croix authorities we were holding Andy pending further investigation."

Millie's heart plummeted. "You can't be serious. Surely you know Andy had nothing to do with Luigi Falco's unfortunate demise."

Donovan Sweeney, who was standing in the far corner, shoved his hands in his front pants pockets. "As soon as the ship sets sail, the captain has full authority over the vessel and he plans to release Andy to return to duty."

"Does Andy know?" she asked.

"Yes. We're waiting for the ship to reach international waters," Patterson confirmed. "But it doesn't mean we aren't in the process of a thorough investigation of Mr. Falco's death.

Unfortunately, it appears Andy was in the wrong place at the wrong time."

Patterson's eyes narrowed as he studied Millie. "In no way does this give you a green light to start your own investigation," he warned. "This is a serious matter. You need to let us get to the bottom of Falco's death."

Millie nodded. "I understand what you're saying," she answered vaguely. "Is it possible the man's death was accidental?"

"As I said before, we are investigating the matter thoroughly, not only to clear Andy's name, but to ensure the safety of all passengers on board the ship."

"I appreciate you sharing that information. There's no way I can fill Andy's shoes," she said as she reached for the door handle.

"You'll need to keep this under your hat," Donovan Sweeney said.

"Of course." Millie nodded and slipped out of the room, closing the door behind her. She slowly made her way down the corridor. The first person she planned to talk to was Andy.

She remembered Annette commenting that Luigi Falco wasn't the most popular employee on board the ship. Could it be someone had overheard Andy and Falco's heated discussion upstairs and saw the perfect opportunity to kill the man and set Andy up as the fall guy?

There was the possibility Luigi Falco's death had been accidental, but Millie felt in her bones that wasn't the case.

If Patterson and his men determined Falco's death wasn't accidental and they were unable to track down Falco's killer, Captain Armati would be forced to turn Andy over to the authorities when the ship docked in Miami.

The ship's seven-day cruise was halfway over. They had already visited San Juan and just left St. Croix. The last port stop would be day after tomorrow when they visited the island of St. Thomas.

Dave Patterson would have to move fast if he planned to solve the mystery of the man's murder before the cruise ended.

Millie decided right then and there that it wouldn't hurt to do a little investigation of her own, as long as she didn't get in the way of Patterson and his men.

Chapter 4

Millie darted from event to event, making sure the ship's activities were rolling along like the well-oiled machine Andy had created. She could have asked some of the other entertainment staff to lend a hand, but Millie didn't want to tip anyone off to Andy's current situation, although she was certain that more than half the crew already knew what was going on.

There were hundreds of crew and staff on board Siren of the Seas, but even with a large crew, it was more like a close-knit community where everyone knew everyone else's business. Not only that, but the higher the ranking, the more the crew seemed to know. The arrest of the ship's cruise director would be big news.

Millie headed to the atrium and noticed the workers were wrapping up the finishing touches on the new karaoke venue.

"We're almost done." Marcus, one of the workers Millie had talked to when she'd stopped by earlier, dropped the wires he was holding. With the tip of his work boot, he nudged them under the edge of the stage.

"It looks fantastic." Millie smiled and nodded to the other workers before she turned her attention to Marcus.

"Yes, Miss Millie. There's enough juice running to these speakers so the passengers on the pool deck will be able to name that tune," he joked.

Millie lifted her eyes and gazed at the glass ceiling as she envisioned the passenger's rendition of Sweet Caroline echoing in the rafters. "Better warn Cat in the gift shop she should stock up on earplugs."

Marcus chuckled. "It will be fun. Perhaps you will sing too?"

Millie shook her head. "You don't want to hear me sing, Marcus. Trust me. Passengers will be jumping ship if they hand me the mike." She changed the subject. "I'm sorry to hear about your co-worker's death."

Marcus' expression grew somber. "Me, too. He married man and leave a wife behind in Cochem," he said in a thick accent.

"Oh, I'm so sorry to hear that," Millie said. She wondered if Mr. Falco's wife had heard the news and offered a small prayer for her, for his entire family.

"But I think she be the only one who is sad," Marcus admitted. "He was a difficult man."

"Was he your boss?" Millie asked.

"Yes." Marcus nodded. "Not for very long. They keep moving him around, you know. He

33

get so many complaints others refuse to work for him."

One of the workers wound the extra cable around his arm and made his way over to Marcus and Millie. "We're all done here," he said.

"We make good time." Marcus turned to Millie. "I will check back later to see if you have any problems. What time does karaoke start?"

"Nine o'clock, on the dot," Millie said.

"I be back a little before nine," Marcus promised.

Millie watched as Marcus and the other workers loaded their tools and equipment onto a small utility cart. After loading the cart, they made their way to the bank of elevators on the other side of the room and then disappeared inside.

She turned her attention to the stage and inspected the equipment one final time before heading upstairs to the pool deck to check on Danielle and the sail away party.

Millie wandered along the railing, picking up empty dinner plates and drink cups as she walked. She stopped near the back of the lido deck and leaned on the railing, watching as the tropical island became a small dot in the distance before it finally disappeared from sight.

The sounds of steel drums echoed from the deck stage as Millie dropped the dirty dishes in the bin near the bar.

"Time to see if Patterson released Andy," she muttered under her breath as she wiped her hands on the front of her work pants and headed down the steps.

The theater was dark. On the other opposite end, Millie could hear the hum of a generator motor, something she'd never noticed before. She wondered if it had something to do with the recent accident.

Millie spied a dim light inside Andy's office and made her way across the stage, her footsteps echoing on the raised stage. "Knock, knock," she said before peeking around the corner.

Andy was seated at the small conference table, his head bent over his black schedule book. He looked up. "Millie."

"Thank God they let you out," Millie said.

"Can't keep a good man down," Andy attempted a smile. "Hopefully Patterson and his men can figure out how Luigi Falco ended up dead outside the theater before we reach Miami. If not..." Andy made a slicing motion across his throat. "I'm history."

"Don't say that," Millie groaned as she pulled a chair out and plopped down. "They can't pin this on you. Yeah, you had a verbal disagreement with the guy hours before his body was found outside your office, but it doesn't mean you did him in."

"It doesn't mean I didn't, either." Andy said.

Millie's eyes widened. "You killed him?"

"No," Andy rolled his eyes. "Of course not."

"Maybe he accidentally electrocuted himself," Millie theorized.

"I thought the same thing." Andy rubbed the faint stubble on his chin. "From what I was told, they found a large electrical burn on the palm of his hand, which means there was juice flowing to the electrical panel he was working on at the time of his death."

"Surely he would have enough sense to shut off the power before working on it." Millie's mind whirled. "Do you think someone turned the power back on and he got zapped?"

"Patterson didn't come right out and say that, but that's what I think happened."

Andy continued. "I was here in my office when the lights flickered and I heard a popping noise. I was the one who got to him first."

"Do you have anyone who can vouch for you? Perhaps one of the dancers was backstage while you were in your office?" Millie asked.

"Not a soul, which makes me the obvious suspect."

Millie leaned back in her chair, crossing her arms in front of her. She gazed at Andy thoughtfully. "It gives you opportunity, but what about motive?"

"Well, therein lies the crux of the whole discombobulated disaster. I filed a complaint against Mr. Falco after our exchange in the atrium and he had done the same, telling Donovan Sweeney I threatened him."

"But you didn't threaten him," Millie said.

"I did say that I thought someone needed to clean his clock and put him in his place." Andy

38

sighed deeply. "One could argue the argument escalated and that I feared my career was in jeopardy."

"That's a stretch," Millie said.

"Is it? People have murdered for a lot less."

Andy had a point. Millie had seen that first hand. She remembered how one of the galley crew had poisoned several of the ship's officers in an attempt to oust a rival and steal her job. "I'm going to start a little investigation of my own."

"I don't think you should do that." Andy shook his head, but he knew from the expression on Millie's face he was wasting his breath. "Patterson won't be happy."

"I know," Millie said. "This Luigi had plenty of enemies. I think someone set you up. They overheard the heated discussion and saw the perfect opportunity to get away with murder."

Andy's radio began to squawk. It was Danielle. "Andy, do you copy?" She sounded frazzled.

Andy picked up his radio. "Yes, Danielle. Go ahead."

"I'm up here on the VIP deck. We've got a little 911 emergency."

"Radio security. I'll be right there." Andy pushed his chair back, clipped his radio to his belt and hurried out of his office. Millie hustled behind him.

When they reached the VIP deck, they found Danielle pacing in front of the bar area.

A sudden movement caught Millie's eye. It was a bikini-clad passenger. She was shimmying barefoot across the gleaming bar top.

Dario, one of the bartenders, lifted his shoulders, as if to say, "I don't know what to do."

"You must come down from there!" Danielle told the woman. "You're going to fall and break your neck."

The woman ignored Danielle's pleas as she continued strutting back and forth.

Millie hurried forward but before she could reach the bar, she watched as the woman lost her footing and her arms began flailing wildly in the air.

Millie squeezed her eyes shut, waiting for the sound of the crash, which never came. She opened her eyes. The woman was dancing again, having apparently regained her footing.

It didn't help that a crowd had gathered and began chanting, "Dance! Dance! Dance!"

Millie tried in vain to quiet the crowd, which only seemed to grow.

Andy hurried to the far end of the bar area and motioned Millie to the other end. "You must get down before we have security remove you from the area and escort you to your cabin," he warned.

It was as if the woman hadn't heard a word Andy said, and she probably hadn't. Judging by her jerky movements, Millie suspected she'd had one too many drinks.

Security arrived on scene moments later and surrounded the bar.

Andy took a step back, unclipped his walkie-talkie, lifted it to his lips and pressed the talk button. "Turn the speakers off in the VIP bar area," he murmured into the radio.

The music that had been blaring out of the speakers above the bar abruptly stopped and so did the woman. "Why'd ja go and turn the music off?" Her words slurred as she shifted sideways and stepped into thin air. Her arms spun in wide circles as she scrambled to regain her footing but it was too late. She was going down.

Felippe, a Siren of the Seas security guard, darted forward and caught the woman midair. He wrapped one arm around the woman's waist and slid his other arm under her legs before he flung her around in a half circle and lowered her to the deck.

The crowd began applauding.

The woman swayed slightly. "I was just getting started."

"You were just finishing," Andy said firmly as he grasped her upper arm and led her out of the area.

"The show is over folks," Millie announced. The crowd dispersed and Millie turned her attention to Dario. "You sure know how to get them engaged."

"Oh Miss Millie." Dario rolled his eyes. "One minute, I mix her a breezy bomb and the next thing I know, she climb on top of the bar and I can't get her down."

Dario grabbed a dishrag and began wiping the smudged footprints from the bar top. "I'm glad to see Mr. Andy is no longer locked up."

"Me too," Millie said. "I think someone is trying to frame him."

"Yes," Dario agreed. "Mr. Andy, he a good man. I say to myself, Dario...I wonder if they talk to Paloma."

"Who is Paloma?" Millie had never heard of Paloma.

"Paloma is...was Luigi Falco's girlfriend."

Chapter 5

"Luigi's girlfriend?" Millie gasped. "She's on this ship?"

"Si." Dario nodded. "She work in housekeeping." He pointed to a set of metal steps behind the bar area. "I see them sneak off down there many times."

Millie stepped over to the railing behind the bar and peered over the side. "What's down there?"

"It's a small storage room, but there another door that lead to the lower level." Dario shrugged. "Most people, they don't know it's there but I see what goes on."

"Have you told anyone else what you just told me?" Millie asked.

Dario shook his head. "Not yet. I work here since early this morning but as soon as I get off work, I stop by and talk to Mr. Patterson. I tell him what I see."

Millie told Dario she agreed and then slowly walked out of the VIP area. Had Luigi's lover killed him?

She wondered if she'd ever seen the girlfriend, Paloma, around the ship. The housekeeping staff worked long hours, starting early in the morning.

Millie knew the housekeeping staff took their breaks in the afternoon and then returned to work in the early evening for turn down service.

When she reached the stairs, she glanced at her wristwatch. Millie had plenty of time before she had to make her way to the karaoke stage. Andy had already touted the new karaoke program over the loudspeakers earlier in the week in an attempt to drum up some excitement. Millie only hoped she could live up to the hype.

Sometimes she believed Andy had too much faith in her.

Technically, this was Millie's break time and she was "off the clock." She made her way to the other side of the ship to the bridge, hoping to not only have a moment to chat with Captain Armati, but also visit with Scout, Captain Armati's teacup Yorkie.

Millie rapped on the outer door leading to the bridge before slipping her keycard into the slot. She waited for the familiar beep and then turned the handle, pushed the door open and slipped inside.

Staff Captain Vitale was standing near the wall of windows overlooking the open ocean. He lowered his binoculars and smiled at Millie as she made her way across the bridge. "Hello Millie. I figured you'd be running around like a chicken with your head cut off today."

Millie smiled. "I would be except they sprung Andy so I was able to sneak in a quick break to say hello to the captain and Scout."

Captain Vitale nodded. "He just stepped into his apartment."

Millie wandered down the small hall that connected the bridge with the captain's private quarters. She had been inside the captain's cabin on numerous occasions, either to pick up Scout so he could accompany her on her daily activities or on special occasions, when the captain had a free evening and invited Millie to dine with him.

She lightly tapped on the outer door and waited for the door to open.

"Ah, Millie. You must've read my mind. I was thinking of you. Come in." The captain swung the door open and motioned her inside, closing the door behind her.

A small brown ball of fur raced across the living room floor and pounced on Millie's shoe.

She reached down and picked up Scout, who promptly licked the side of her chin and then pawed at her dangling earring.

She moved the earring out of his reach and nuzzled the top of Scout's head. "I guess you didn't miss me." Millie hadn't seen Scout in a couple of days, not since the ship had sailed from Miami.

Scout wiggled and squirmed, his whole body shaking. Millie gently set him on the floor where he raced over to his box of toys and bit the neck of a yellow giraffe she'd picked up for him a couple weeks earlier.

He dragged it across the room and dropped it at her feet. "Thank you, Scout, for sharing your toys." She patted his head and then straightened her back. "I thought I would stop by to say hello and also check to see if you're still hosting dinner at the captain's table this evening."

"Yes." Captain Armati nodded. "Patterson is on top of Mr. Falco's murder investigation and I see no reason to punish staff, including Andy, for an unfortunate incident."

"I think Andy was set up," Millie said. "Did you know Mr. Falco was not well-liked by his staff and that he also had a girlfriend on board?"

Captain Armati raised an eyebrow. "Really? I knew he was not well-liked, but this is the first I've heard of the other."

Millie proceeded to tell him what Dario had told her. When she finished, he told her he would be sure Dave Patterson was apprised of the new information.

"Dario told me he was going to stop by Patterson's office after his shift ended," Millie said.

Captain Armati touched Millie's arm lightly. "Can I get you something to drink, Millie? A glass of tea? Bottled water?"

"No thanks." Millie shook her head. "I can't stay long. I'm in charge of the new karaoke program later tonight, somewhat appropriately named "Killer Karaoke." She grimaced.

"The other reason I'm here is to ask permission for a special guest to board the ship when we dock in St. Thomas." She explained to Captain Armati how Annette and she had tried to coax Cat off the ship and had failed miserably.

"I'm worried the longer she remains on board the ship, the less likely we are to ever get her off again," Millie said, "so I contacted a psychologist. I haven't heard back since the ship sailed and now I don't have cell service."

Captain Armati placed both hands behind his back. "I appreciate your concern for your friend. Cat has been through a lot. You have my permission. You'll need to make sure the woman is off the ship before we leave St. Thomas."

"I'll personally escort her both on and off the ship," Millie promised.

Captain Armati's expression grew serious. "I have something important to discuss with you."

Millie's heart skipped a beat and her cheeks warmed as he took a step closer. "Yes?"

He opened his mouth to speak, closed it, and then opened it again. "I...don't think we'll have time to snorkel in St. Thomas."

"I understand," Millie said. "Between Andy's crisis and Cat's intervention, I think we'll have our hands full. Maybe next time we visit the island." She patted Scout's head. "I better get back to work before Andy sends out a search party."

Scout followed her across the room and into the hall. He knew she was leaving and let out a small *yip*.

Millie picked him up and tucked him in the crook of her arm. "Scout hasn't been out in a few days. Do you mind if he makes a few rounds with me? I'll bring him back before heading down for dinner."

"Yes. Of course." Captain Armati led Millie and Scout to the door. He reached for the handle and then tipped his head, as if he was going to kiss her but at the last minute, pulled back, the expression on his face unreadable. "I'll see you later."

Captain Armati opened the door and Millie and Scout stepped into the hall. She nodded to Captain Vitale before exiting the bridge.

When they reached the main hall, Millie pulled the door shut behind her, all the while wondering what had just happened.

***

Scout was on his best behavior as they passed through the fitness center, which was empty. The next stop was the sun deck. They circled around the mini golf course and headed to *Ocean Oasis*, the small area the captain and the maintenance crew had constructed for Millie and Scout.

Millie began filling Scout's pint-size pool with fresh water. The small pup was so excited, he jumped in and began splashing around before she could finish filling it. She could almost see the smile on Scout's face as he darted back and forth.

Millie plucked one of his balls from the small bin inside the area and they played catch for a few minutes. "Okay Scout. We have to get back to work." Millie dropped the ball in the bin and reached for a towel on the nearby rack.

Scout hopped out of the pool and raced to the corner. Millie chased after him. "I know you don't want to go, but we have to." She quickly towel-dried him, pulled the drain from the pool and then hung the wet towel on a hook to dry.

"Let's head to deck nine to see if any of the Siren Sailors are there." Siren Sailors was the nickname for the 8 – 12 year-olds on board the ship. Scout and she visited them every so often and the kids loved seeing Scout as much as he loved seeing them.

Bright, neon colors covered the walls of the Siren Sailors' activity room. Inside the room were several large, flat screen television sets, stacks of video game consoles, as well as an air hockey table and foosball table. There was even a snack bar.

The blips and beeps of the video games echoed through the open door. She set Scout on the floor and he led the way into the room. He trotted over to a group of kids who were sprawled out on bean bag chairs, playing video games.

Two of the girls dropped their controls, rolled onto their knees and began playing with Scout.

Millie stood off to the side and watched for several long moments before she glanced at her watch. They had to keep moving. "C'mon, Scout. We gotta head home."

When Scout and Millie reached the bridge, Captain Armati and Captain Vitale were nowhere in sight. There were two other crewmembers operating the controls. Millie had seen them before but couldn't remember their names.

She headed down the hall to the captain's apartment. Millie knocked on the door and when no one answered, she punched in the access code on the keypad box above the door handle.

She eased the door open, just far enough for Scout to slip inside, before closing it behind him. It was time to head back to her cabin to get ready for the formal dinner.

Millie spent a little extra time primping for the Captain's Dinner. She'd only dined at his table on one other occasion and it had been months ago, right after she joined the staff.

Her hair was getting long and she deftly smoothed it into a chic chignon. Millie turned her head from side to side as she studied what she determined were a new set of wrinkles around the corners of her eyes and the sides of her mouth.

Millie tugged on the bottom of her skirt, slipped her feet into her only pair of heels and exited her small cabin.

The Blue Seas dining room was teeming with passengers and wait staff. Millie nodded to several familiar faces as she circled the room and made her way to the captain's table.

Andy and Captain Armati were already there, as well as two other couples Millie assumed were passengers.

The men stood as Millie approached, and Captain Armati pulled out an empty chair next to his. He waited for her to sit before sliding it back in.

The other men resumed their places after Millie was seated. She unfolded her napkin and placed it in her lap as she shot the captain a furtive glance out of the corner of her eye. She remembered the odd exchange earlier and once again, Millie wondered what it meant.

She had a feeling he was going to tell her something, and it had nothing to do with him having to postpone their snorkeling excursion in St. Thomas.

It was something else. Perhaps he had met someone else and didn't know how to tell her. She shoved the thought aside. Surely, she would've heard that rumor buzzing around the ship, but then again, maybe not since many of the crew knew she and the captain were an "item."

The conversation flowed freely and the food was delicious. Formal night offerings included surf and turf and Millie enjoyed the lobster. She smiled when she remembered the first time she'd dined in the captain's apartment and tasted lobster.

Captain Armati...Nic...had expertly shown her how to remove the lobster from the shell.

After the appetizers, salad and main course had been served, coffee and a dessert tray arrived. Millie skipped dessert, still full from the big meal.

Andy sipped his coffee as he questioned the passengers about the ship's activities, anxious to get their honest feedback. They assured both Andy and Millie that they were thoroughly enjoying the fun-filled days on board the ship.

After Andy finished his coffee, he reluctantly stood. "It's time to get back to work."

Millie followed suit. "The show must go on," she quipped and then turned to the captain. "I had a lovely evening. Thank you for inviting me." She shifted her gaze and smiled at the passengers, still seated at the table. "It was a pleasure meeting you and I hope you enjoy the rest of your cruise."

Andy made his way around the table as he shook the passengers' hands. He approached Captain Armati last, taking his hand in a firm grip. "Rumor has it you're jumping ship and moving to Baroness of the Seas next month."

Chapter 6

Millie gripped the back of her chair and the room began to spin. She swayed slightly. *Captain Armati was leaving Siren of the Seas?*

Andy must've noticed the stricken look on Millie's face. "Millie...I didn't."

Millie forced a weak smile. "Good luck, Captain Armati. Baroness of the Seas will be lucky to have you," she croaked.

She wasn't sure how she managed it, but Millie held her head high as she strode out of the dining room and down the side stairs. She didn't stop until she reached the safety of her cabin where she darted inside, slamming the door behind her.

She leaned her forehead against the back of the door and closed her eyes.

"Millie! Let me in." The door began to shake as Andy pounded on it.

Millie ignored the pounding and after a couple minutes, it stopped.

In a daze, she slipped out of her eveningwear and changed back into her uniform. Why hadn't Nic...Captain Armati told her?

It dawned on her that was what he was about to tell her up in his apartment, but for some reason, he didn't. Instead, she had to hear the devastating news in front of a room full of strangers.

Nic had assured her a couple months back that he had no intention of leaving Siren of the Seas or leaving her. Had he lied to her and strung her along, all the while planning his departure?

If that was the kind of person he was, she wanted nothing to do with him!

Millie thought of her ex-husband, Roger. They had been married for what she thought were 38 happy years when she discovered he'd been cheating on her with one of his clients, Delilah Osborne.

Roger had been one of the reasons Millie had applied for the assistant cruise director position aboard Siren of the Seas in the first place, to escape the heartbreak and unbearable pain of her failed marriage.

She'd almost believed happiness could be hers again. Captain Armati was her knight in shining armor. He was everything Millie was looking for...handsome, smart, warm, caring and thoughtful.

Millie's eyes burned with unshed tears and the pit of her stomach churned, as a wave of betrayal washed over her. She shuffled over to the small desk in the corner, reached inside the drawer and pulled out her worn Bible. She flipped to one of her favorite Bible verses, Romans 8:18 KJV:

"For I reckon that the sufferings of this present time are not worthy to be compared with the glory which shall be revealed in us."

Millie repeated the verse, closed her eyes and prayed the Lord would help her through the rest of the evening. She prayed for her children, her family, for Cat and for Andy.

She opened her eyes, quietly closed her Bible, slipped it back inside the drawer and walked out of the cabin.

***

Millie adjusted the mike stand in front of the small stage and then pulled the microphone from the holder before she switched it on. "Testing. Give me a wave if you can hear me."

Several passengers waved. She shut the microphone off and then turned her attention to Felix, one of the dancers who had volunteered to co-host the new, debut "Killer Karaoke" program.

The evening theater show, "Gem of the Seas," had ended and guests began making their way into the atrium, lining the upper floor balconies that circled the atrium.

Millie turned to Felix. "It's time to fire up the crowd." She switched the microphone on again.

"Welcome to our brand spanking new event, *Killer Karaoke.*" Millie gazed at the growing crowd. "This is a passenger participation event so those of you who would like to impress your fellow passengers, not to mention your family and friends, with not only your trivia knowledge, but also your stellar singing abilities, gather round."

She waved the crowds forward and several groups of people crowded around the front of the small stage.

Felix handed Millie a manila file folder. She reached for her reading glasses and slipped them on. "Gotta have those glasses."

"Killer Karaoke is a new spin on an oldie but a goodie. My partner, Felix, will play a small clip of a song and the first one to correctly guess either the name of the song or the artist who sings it, will then get to sing the song, and if you're lucky, we'll all sing along."

She continued. "The first five participants will receive...drum roll please, Sir Felix."

Felix rolled his eyes and then rolled his tongue as he mimicked a drum roll.

"Will receive a free drink coupon, which can be used at any bar on the ship as well as the specialty coffee shop located on deck seven."

Felix turned to face the instrument panel. He flipped the switch for a brief second and a few bars of a popular pop song blared through the loudspeakers.

"Happy!" A girl in the crowd shrieked.

Millie smiled. "You are correct." The girl ran onto the stage and Millie shifted the microphone toward her. "What's your name dear?"

"Piper."

"Well, Piper. You have a sharp ear. Now it's your turn to sing."

The girl nodded excitedly as Millie handed her the microphone. She pointed to the small screen at the front of the stage that displayed the words to the song before stepping off the stage.

The music began to play and the girl began to sing her heart out, almost completely on key. Throngs of passengers joined in and the happy voices echoed to the rafters.

When she finished the song, the crowd gave her a standing ovation, perhaps because they were standing.

Millie presented her with the gift certificate. The girl clutched her gift certificate and skipped off the stage.

The rest of the evening flew by and crowd participation was higher than Millie had ever seen it.

Andy swung by halfway through, grinning from ear to ear at the successful launch of the new and improved karaoke event.

After the last song ended and Felix and she put everything away, Millie headed to the buffet area. It was closed for the evening, but the 24-hour pizza station in the back was busy, as well as the deli station.

Millie ordered a slice of pepperoni pizza, stopped by the drink station for a watered down glass of lemonade and then made her way to a table in the corner.

Andy must've had the same idea as he wandered into the area moments later. He gave a small wave before stopping by the pizza station.

"So this is where you're hiding out. Mind if I join you?" he asked as he slid his plate of pizza and stack of breadsticks onto the table.

"Of course not," Millie said between bites. She watched as he walked over to the drink station, returning with the same watered down lemonade she'd gotten.

"It's not very good." She pointed to the glass of lemonade.

"Thanks for the warning." Andy eased into the seat across from Millie. "Karaoke was a huge success," he said as he reached for a breadstick.

"The passengers loved it," Millie agreed. They discussed their new endeavor and then the conversation drifted to Luigi Falco's death.

Millie plucked a pepperoni from the top of her pizza and popped it into her mouth. "Did you know Luigi had a girlfriend on board?"

She told Andy what Dario had told her. "I think she is a suspect, as well as some of Luigi's co-workers and other crew."

"Not to mention someone even higher up on the totem pole, even higher than me," Andy said quietly.

"Who's that?" Millie asked.

"Captain Armati."

Chapter 7

Millie's jaw dropped. "You're kidding."

"I wish I was." Andy dipped the end of his breadstick in marinara sauce and then took a big bite. "I know for a fact the captain recently demoted Luigi Falco and placed him on probation. Luigi got ticked and lodged a formal complaint."

The pieces of the puzzle were beginning to fall into place. "Is that why Captain Armati is transferring to another ship?"

"I hope not, but I don't know for sure," Andy shrugged.

Millie bit the end of her pizza slice and chewed thoughtfully. "I'm sure other crewmembers have lodged complaints in the past. Do you think Captain Armati is trying to hide something?"

"I don't know all the details. There may be more to Captain Armati's request to move to another ship," Andy confessed. "All I know is Captain Armati's transfer request was approved and he's leaving soon, unless, of course, higher ups decide to put the transfer on hold, while Mr. Falco's death is being investigated."

Either way, it didn't look promising for Millie and Captain Armati.

Millie stared at the half-eaten pizza on her plate. Her appetite vanished and she pushed the plate away.

Apparently, Andy's brief lock up hadn't affected his appetite and he bit into his pizza with gusto.

He went on. "Look, Millie. I can see the wheels turning in your head, that you think if you figure out who murdered Falco, the captain will withdraw his request. I will be off the hook and we'll all live happily ever after aboard the Siren of the Seas."

"So?" Millie asked. "What's wrong with that? You're like family, which means I'll do whatever I can to help track down the killer and clear your name."

Andy was already shaking his head. "I appreciate your loyalty and wanting to help, but the only thing you're going to do is end up getting into hot water. For once, perhaps you should leave it to the investigators."

Millie didn't reply. She was already mapping out a plan to uncover the killer.

***

Annette twirled the knife around the edge of the layered black forest cake and eyed Millie. "I heard the rumor Captain Armati was jumping ship, but had no idea why. I don't blame you for wanting to get to the bottom of this. I'm sure the last thing you want is for him to leave."

"I don't want him to leave and I definitely don't want him or Andy to be charged with

73

Falco's murder." Millie rested her chin on her fisted hand and gazed absentmindedly at the cake.

Annette paused and pointed the tip of her knife at Millie. "I'd check to see if there are cameras outside the theater and if so, if they caught any suspicious activity around the time of Falco's death."

"Done," Millie said. "I swung by there on my way here. There are cameras but they're pointed down the hall, not at the breaker box just inside the door. Plus, the area is roped off. I'm sure Dave Patterson has already viewed the video footage and would have found something if it had recorded."

"What about Andy? Did he hear or see anything suspicious right before Falco's death?"

"Negative." Millie shook her head. "Other than a flicker of the lights followed by a popping noise at the precise moment Falco got zapped. That's how he found him."

Annette set the knife on the countertop and reached for a jar of cherries. She unscrewed the lid and grabbed a spoon before scooping out a handful and then carefully arranging them along the top of the cake. "We need a list of suspects, other than Andy and Captain Armati."

She scooped out another handful. "If this Falco guy had run-ins with Armati and Andy, surely he had run-ins with others, workers who were close to him."

"I need someone on the inside that I can talk to," Millie said. She remembered Marcus, the electrician who had helped her set the stage for the new activity, Killer Karaoke. "I have an idea."

Millie hopped off the barstool and then pushed it under the counter. "I'm going to disconnect a couple wires from the karaoke set up and then ask Marcus, the electrician who helped set it up, to come down. While he's there, I'll pump him for information."

With a plan in place, Millie exited the galley and made a beeline for deck five. There were a few late night stragglers hanging out at the atrium bar.

She hurried to the back of the stage, behind the curtain and studied the clusters of wires. "This looks as good as any." Millie bent down, grabbed a wire that led to the microphone and pulled. The cable disconnected at the joint and Millie dropped it on the floor before glancing at her watch. It was too late to call Marcus, but Millie vowed to stop by first thing in the morning to "check" on the equipment and then give him a call.

It was time for Millie to make her final rounds. Her first stop was to check in with Bobby, the bartender, who worked in the Tahitian Nights Dance Club.

Her next stop was Paradise Lounge, the comedy club. The late night, adults-only show was in full swing and the lounge packed. She stood near the door and listened for a moment before backing out of the room and making her way to the piano bar.

Millie heard the piano bar before she saw it, as guests and the host belted out a rousing rendition of *Brown-eyed Girl*. She peeked inside. The piano player, Joey, gave Millie a quick nod.

After she'd finished all of her rounds, Millie headed to the galley to chat with Annette but the lights were off and the door locked. There was nothing left to do except head back to her cabin. Tomorrow would be another busy day at sea and Millie was scheduled to participate in the Early Risers Sunrise Stretch at 7:30 in the gym.

Millie slipped her keycard into the door slot and waited for the beep before pushing the cabin door open and stepping inside.

"Hello? Danielle?" The cabin was dark. She flipped on the lights and then waited, giving her eyes a moment to adjust to the bright lights.

Danielle, her cabin mate, was nowhere in sight.

Millie hung her lanyard on the hook near the door, kicked her shoes off, nudging them under her bed and then lifted her hands over her head in a long stretch as she yawned loudly.

The door suddenly flew open and Danielle exploded into the room. "Good golly, Miss Molly! You'll never guess what I just saw."

Chapter 8

Millie dropped her hands and clutched her chest. "You scared me half to death. What if I had been asleep?"

"Sorry." Danielle slowly closed the cabin door. "I wasn't thinking."

Millie slumped onto the edge of the bed and eyed her roommate cautiously. "What did you just see?"

"I was up in Waves, checking on the late night Chocolate Extravaganza," Danielle said.

Millie interrupted as she pointed at the dinner napkin Danielle was holding. "And sampling the goodies?"

Danielle turned the napkin over in her hand. "Of course. Gotta make sure the food is up to snuff, especially the late night treats. Don't want the kitchen crew cutting corners, thinking no one is paying attention."

"How admirable of you," Millie said wryly. "I trust you found the chocolate acceptable?"

"Yep." Danielle unfolded the napkin and held it out. "I took a couple extra chocolate-covered caramel nut cookies. You want to try one?"

Millie shook her head. "No thanks. I'm still full from the pizza I ate a short time ago, not to mention a big dinner. So what happened?" she prompted.

"I finished circling the chocolate displays and was getting ready to head to the pool area when I spotted Dave Patterson talking to Lorenzo, the new guy I introduced you to." Danielle moseyed over to the small desk, pulled out the chair and plopped down before nibbling the edge of one of the cookies. "Don't you think that's odd?"

"I'm sure Patterson is interviewing crew and staff since he's investigating Luigi Falco's death.

Why he would be talking to a new housekeeping staff is anyone's guess, unless Lorenzo thought he saw something."

"True." Danielle popped the rest of the cookie in her mouth, folded the napkin to cover the remaining cookie and then placed it on the desk. "So when are you starting the investigation?"

"What investigation?"

Danielle lifted an eyebrow. "You know what investigation. Falco's murder and don't tell me that you're not."

"I was told to stay out of it," Millie said, which was the honest to goodness truth.

"But you're not going to, not when it involves two people you care about, Captain Armati and Andy." Danielle drummed her fingers on the desktop. "I heard the dead guy was a real jerk so we have plenty of motive, but opportunity, that's the real zinger. The fact it happened right outside the theater, not long after the deceased

81

argued with Andy, and Andy was the one to discover his body puts him in the hot seat."

"We both know it was a set up," Millie said. "Andy is the fall guy and someone is hoping to get away with murder." She slowly stood and headed to the closet where she pulled out her pajamas and then made her way to the bathroom door.

Danielle mumbled a reply.

Millie grabbed the door handle. "What did you say?"

"Nothing," Danielle said. "Just thinking out loud."

When Millie emerged from the bathroom a short time later, Danielle began waving a piece of paper in the air. "I jotted down a list of suspects."

Millie opened the closet door and tossed her dirty uniform in her laundry basket before wandering over to Danielle. "I need my reading glasses." She reached inside the top drawer, pulled out her glasses and slipped them on.

Danielle handed her the sheet of paper:

Andy, Captain Armati, everyone in the electrical department, the girlfriend.

Millie handed the sheet back to Danielle. "I would put the girlfriend, Paloma, at the top of the list, followed by the entire electrical department and then Andy and Captain Armati at the bottom."

Millie placed her reading glasses inside the drawer before she crawled into bed, pulling the covers to her chin. "You should get ready for bed. Tomorrow is going to be a busy day and I have to be upstairs at the crack of dawn for the early risers."

Danielle hopped out of the chair and headed to the bathroom. "I think I figured out why Patterson was talking to Lorenzo tonight."

Millie switched her small nightlight on. "Why?"

"Lorenzo works in housekeeping."

"Yeah?"

"Well, every new staff member has to start at the bottom, which means Lorenzo's first assignment would include cleaning certain common areas before being promoted to passenger cabins."

"So you think Lorenzo may have been working outside the theater?" Millie said.

"Maybe. I'll talk to him tomorrow," Danielle said before slipping into the tiny bathroom and closing the door behind her.

Millie stared at the bathroom door before switching off her night light. Between the two of them, maybe they could stumble upon some sort of clue.

She closed her eyes and prayed the killer would be brought to justice, Andy and Captain Armati would be cleared and the captain would not transfer to another ship.

***

The next morning, Millie was awake before the alarm sounded. She wasn't sure why or what had woken her, at least not until she heard humming coming from the bathroom.

Millie was always suspicious when Danielle, who was definitely not a morning person, was up and around before she was, especially when she didn't have to be.

She flipped her small bedside light on and flung a hand over her eyes as she attempted to focus.

"Rise and shine sleepyhead," Danielle chirped merrily as she emerged from the bathroom, dressed and ready to start her day.

"Let me guess. You spent the night in the bathroom," Millie joked as she flung the covers back and swung her legs off the side of the bed.

"Nah. I couldn't sleep last night, thinking about Captain Armati and Andy's predicament. It's such a shame."

Millie slid out of her bunk. "Could it also have something to do with the fact you're trying to get that job in the bridge and if Captain Armati transfers to another ship, your chances of moving into that position are sunk?"

Ingrid Kozlov, one of the crew who worked alongside Captain Armati and Staff Captain Antonio Vitale in the bridge, had recently been fired.

Ingrid had never cared for Millie and she always secretly believed Ingrid had a crush on the captain and was jealous of their relationship.

"Maybe," Danielle hedged. "I mean, it's the perfect position for me, other than possibly working in security. I was hoping to try my hand at a few different positions to figure out where I fit best."

In the beginning, Danielle had annoyed Millie, but the young woman was growing on her and she had to admit she'd grown fond of her.

Danielle's history was a mystery. The only thing Millie knew was the young woman had previously worked as an undercover agent, held a black belt in karate and somehow managed to get into more trouble than Millie did.

On several occasions, Danielle had woken Millie in the dead of the night, after having had a nightmare. During the last episode, Millie had heard the name "Casey." She hadn't pressed Danielle, but whoever "Casey" was, was an important person to Danielle.

"I'm going to take a run through the crew quarters to see if I can track down Lorenzo." Danielle slipped her lanyard over her head, and then flipped her blonde locks over her shoulder before inspecting her reflection in the mirror. "I'll let you know if I find anything out."

Millie waited until the cabin door closed behind Danielle before heading to the bathroom. She quickly showered, pulled her hair in a tight bun and then slipped into a pair of sweatpants and t-shirt.

She decided to grab a bite to eat after the early risers' class and was one of the first to arrive in the gym. Alison Coulter, one of the dancers, was in charge of the class. She smiled when Millie wandered into the room and plopped down on an empty floor mat.

Millie eased onto her back and stared up at the ceiling before closing her eyes. "Have mercy on me this morning, Alison. I'm feeling a little creaky in my old age."

Alison snorted. "Creaky my foot. You're in better shape than half of the dancers."

Millie lifted her head and peered at her young friend. "You think so?"

"Of course," Alison smiled. "I'm surprised Andy doesn't put you in charge of the class."

"Oh no," Millie groaned. "Don't you dare plant that idea in his head."

Passengers began wandering in, carrying Styrofoam cups of coffee and taking their places on the empty mats. The room filled and Millie was surprised at how many passengers, almost all women, were up early.

After everyone took their place, Alison switched the CD player on and a catchy, upbeat jazz song blared through the speakers. The forty-minute workout flew by and when it was over, Millie's limbs were loose and she was wide-awake.

She thanked Alison for a great workout before heading to the women's locker room for a quick shower and to change out of her workout clothes and into her uniform. She had finished showering and dressing and was about to step out of the dressing room when she caught murmured voices and Captain Armati's name.

Millie released her grip on the door handle. She took a step back as she held her breath and listened. "...with Captain Armati."

"Or maybe Luigi's boss, Carmine, had something to do with Luigi's death," another female replied. "Paloma told me he was sending her notes and it was creeping her out."

The voices drifted away as the female crewmembers exited the changing room. Millie's heart began to pound. She'd heard the chief electrician's name before, neither good nor bad, just that he ran a tight ship in the electrical department, a critical function on all cruise ships.

What if the chief electrician and Luigi had argued and Carmine, seeing his opportunity to commit the near-perfect crime, set Andy up...or even Captain Armati? Meanwhile, he got away with murder and ended up with the dead man's girlfriend.

Millie hurried from the locker room. She made a pit stop in the buffet area for a quick breakfast consisting of an English muffin, slice of sharp cheddar cheese, a small scoop of scrambled eggs and a couple slices of crispy bacon.

She headed to a small bistro table outdoors where she assembled her makeshift sandwich. Millie bowed her head and closed her eyes. She prayed for a good day. When she finished praying, she lifted her head and stared out at the tranquil seas before picking up her sandwich and taking a bite.

Her next order of business was to head down to the karaoke stage to make sure the mic was still disconnected and the wires shoved under the edge of the stage before she called in the electricians to give her a hand and hopefully a few clues.

Chapter 9

"I don't understand." Marcus shook his head and stared at the tangled cords. "It work fine yesterday." His shoulders slumped. "This might take some time to figure out." He plucked his radio from his belt, lifted it to his lips and pressed the button. "Filip. Do you copy?"

The radio crackled. "Go ahead Marcus."

"I need help on deck five by the karaoke," Marcus said. "The equipment, it not working."

There was a long moment of silence. "I be right there," a clipped voice replied.

"We fix you up in no time," Marcus assured Millie.

"I appreciate your help," Millie said. "I'm sure you're even busier now that Mr. Falco is gone."

"Yes." Marcus nodded. "But uh..."

She could see him search for the right words. "We be all right. Mr. Carmine, he make sure we get work done."

"Ah," Millie said. "Mr. Carmine is in charge of your department, even higher than Mr. Falco's position."

"Yes," Marcus agreed. "Carmine, he a good man but Mr. Falco, no so much. They argue but maybe it have something to do with..." Marcus' voice trailed off.

Millie was losing him! "Paloma," she blurted out. "The men were arguing over Paloma."

"Yes." Marcus glanced around and then leaned in. "I heard Mr. Carmine threaten to contact Falco's wife to tell her about girlfriend, Paloma."

"I wonder what Paloma thought of that," Millie mused.

"Ah. She no care. She go around telling everyone she tell the missus herself. Luigi and her, they get in big fight. Women." Marcus shrugged his shoulders.

The other worker, Filip, arrived on scene and the conversation ended. Millie attempted to lead them toward the wires she had disconnected the night before. She finally gave up and pointed out where the "disconnect" was located as she held up the wires. "Shouldn't this be plugged in?"

Marcus hurried over and took the wire from Millie. "Yes, but I thought I already check this wire."

Millie waved her hand at the thick roll of jumbled wires. "It would be easy to miss with all of these."

Marcus snapped the ends together and Millie made her way over to the microphone. She flipped the switch. "Testing, testing." Her voice echoed in the atrium and several passengers waved.

"You fixed it." Millie shut the microphone off and grinned at Marcus.

"You fixed it Miss Millie. Maybe we should hire you in our department," Marcus joked.

The men packed up their toolboxes and headed for the stairs.

After they were gone, Millie wandered over to the guest services counter. Nikki Tan smiled as Millie approached. "I caught the beginning of last night's karaoke. You did a great job and the guests were rocking it out."

"Thanks." Millie propped her elbow on the counter and casually cased the room. "I need to track down an employee who works in housekeeping. I only have her first name, though. Paloma."

"Ah." Nikki lifted an eyebrow. "So you are on the case." She shifted her attention to the computer in front of her and began tapping on the keys. "Yes. Paloma works on deck eleven,

95

the panorama deck.   It looks as if she cleans the suites near the front of the ship."

Millie nodded. "I'm familiar with the section. My cousins, Gloria and Liz, cruised a few months back and they both had suites on the panorama deck. Thanks for the info." She patted the top of the counter and then turned to leave.

"Millie."

Millie turned back.

"I don't want Captain Armati to leave either," Nikki said softly. "It would be like losing a family member."

Millie blinked back unexpected tears and swallowed hard. "I think so too, Nikki," she whispered. "I think so, too."

***

The suite area of the panorama deck was empty except for a cleaning cart and a young woman who was holding a clipboard, inspecting the cart's contents. "Paloma?"

The woman took a step back and turned. Whatever Millie expected Paloma to look like...this wasn't it. She was young, a lot younger than Luigi Falco.

"Yes?"

"I'm Millie Sanders, Assistant Cruise Director. I wondered if you had a moment to chat with me."

The girl slowly nodded and a long dark strand of hair fell across her face. "Of course. You work with Andy, Mr. Walker," Paloma said.

"I do," Millie replied, "which is one of the reasons why I'm here. I'd like to ask you a couple questions about Luigi Falco."

The woman's brown eyes widened. "I...Mr. Patterson already talked to me."

She continued. "I had nothing to do with Luigi's death."

"From what I've heard, Luigi had many enemies, including his own boss, Mr. Carmine."

The young woman's mouth formed an "o" and she tightened her grip on the clipboard she was holding.

Millie pressed on. "Did Luigi ever mention arguing with Mr. Carmine, Mr. Walker or the captain?"

"He mentioned their names, that they tried to have him fired so he filed a complaint," Paloma said.

Millie had to wonder how on earth the attractive young woman standing in front of her had managed to become involved with a much older, married man who was disliked by so many of the ship's crew. Perhaps it was a sense of security, or maybe he had promised her a promotion.

A young crewmember, carrying a vacuum cleaner emerged from a cabin three doors down.

"I must get back to work." Paloma scurried into one of the suites and disappeared from sight.

Millie nodded to the young man and then retraced her steps. When she reached the end of the hall, she stopped. Something told her Paloma knew more than she let on.

When she reached the end of the hall, Millie studied her surroundings. There was a women's restroom near the stairwell. She slipped inside, leaving the door open a fraction of an inch, just enough so she could keep an eye on the hall.

Moments later, Paloma darted into the stairwell. She glanced around nervously before grabbing the handrail and descending the steps.

Millie sprang into action as she eased the door open and tiptoed across the hall. She peered over the stairwell and caught a glimpse of the top of Paloma's head.

The steps were steep and Millie took them two at a time in an attempt to trail Paloma but by the time Millie reached the deck where she'd last seen the woman, she had vanished into thin air.

Chapter 10

"I do love a good stakeout," Annette said.

"Me too. I need to take my mind off being cooped up on this ship," Cat added.

"That's..."

Cat held up a hand. "I know. It's my fault. I'm working on it." She changed the subject. "So what's the plan? You think this Paloma chick knows more about Luigi Franco's death than she's letting on and now you want to track her every move?"

Millie wrinkled her nose. "I don't know about every move. I have a strong hunch about her."

"Or maybe you're grasping at straws, desperate to make a connection," Annette said. "Either way, I'm in. I have something that may make our gumshoe operation a little less tedious. Be right back."

Annette disappeared through the side galley door.

Millie turned her attention to her friend, Cat. "You've been avoiding us," she said bluntly.

Cat lowered her gaze and rubbed an imaginary speck on the galley countertop. "Maybe," she admitted. "I feel guilty, knowing I let you and Annette down the other day when I promised to walk as far as the dock, but when I got there, I panicked. I thought I was going to pass out."

Millie was on the fence about telling Cat that Annette and she had decided to contact a local psychologist they hoped could meet with Cat when they reached the island of St. Thomas. She wasn't sure how Cat would react so she attempted to broach the subject.

"How do you feel about talking to a professional, someone who can help you work through your feelings instead of being pressured by two friends who are trying to force you out of your funk?"

Cat twirled her finger in a circular motion near her temple. "You mean like a cuckoo doctor? A shrink?"

"A psychologist...a woman," Millie said. "What if I told you I was able to get an okay to bring her on board so you wouldn't have to get off the ship?"

Cat gazed at Millie thoughtfully. "I dunno..."

"Don't say no yet. Think about it," Millie insisted.

The galley door swung open and Annette sauntered back into the kitchen. She slid a black box with a set of headphones on top of the counter. "I think we oughta start with this."

"What is it?"

"A wiretap."

"Where did you get that?" Millie waved a dismissive hand. "Never mind. I probably don't want to know."

Annette pulled a small device from her front pocket and held it up for inspection. "All we gotta do is attach this baby to Paloma's cleaning cart and we can listen to every single word she says."

Millie frowned. "It could take time to hear anything. We don't have a lot of time. We need to uncover the killer before we dock in Miami."

"You have a better plan?" Annette set the small device on top of the black box.

"I do. I think we should sneak into Paloma's cabin and search it," Millie said.

"It sounds risky." Cat frowned. "What about her cabin mate? What if we get caught?"

"All we gotta do is get our hands on Paloma and her cabin mate's shift schedule. While they're at work, we sneak in and search the place."

"Just like that." Annette snapped her fingers.

"Kind of. I haven't worked out the details yet," Millie admitted. "We could bribe the head room steward to get the information. I'm sure the crew who work in the same department, bunk together. I would think Paloma's cabin mate also works in housekeeping."

"True," Annette agreed. "Maybe we could do a little 'greasing of the palms.'" She rubbed her thumb across her other fingers. "Cold hard cash to take a look at Paloma and her cabin mate's shift schedule."

"First we have to figure out who shares her cabin," Cat said.

"That's easy enough. Who is the biggest gossip and nosiest person on board this ship?" Millie asked.

"Rachel Quaid," Cat and Annette said in unison. Rachel Quaid had joined the crew aboard Siren of the Seas a few months back. She nearly managed to get herself fired her second day on the job after attempting to dig up some dirt on Donovan Sweeney by sucking up to the staff at guest services, Donovan's close-knit group of employees.

Nikki Tan ratted Rachel out, which had nearly turned into a knockdown, drag-out brawl behind the guest services desk. Brody, one of the ship's bouncers, happened to be passing by when it started and stepped in to break up the hair-pulling, face-slapping scuffle.

It was the talk of the ship until the next big thing came along, but Rachel's busybody reputation grew as she planted her nose firmly in everyone's business. It may not have been a huge issue had it not been for the fact the woman had access to a lot of the crew and staff's private information. She was the ship's nurse.

"We need someone who can get her to talk."
Millie had only met the woman in passing.

Annette and Millie eyed Cat, who was close to
Doctor Gundervan, Rachel's boss.

"Oh, don't look at me." Cat shook her head. "I
try to avoid the woman at all costs. She's already
trying to psychoanalyze me and ruin, I mean, run
my life."

"But she does like you," Annette pointed out.
"Which means you may be able to get the insider
scoop on Paloma."

Two sets of eyes gazed at Cat intently. "All
right," she caved. "But if she tries to hypnotize
me again, that's it. You're on your own."

Cat popped off the stool and muttered under
her breath. "I have no idea how you two manage
to talk me into some of this stuff."

"While you head down to the medical center, I
need to get my trivia contest under way," Millie
said.

"And I need to work on tomorrow's menu," Annette said.

"I'll report back later," Cat promised.

The trio separated and Millie headed up to the seating area outside the casino. It was the official location for trivia and Andy had recently given Millie free reign to tinker with the trivia contest questions.

So far, she'd tried a Caribbean islands trivia contest, which had been a huge hit, as well as a Majestic Cruise lines trivia contest.

Today, she was going to play it safe, and decided to host a sports trivia, followed by a movie trivia.

Andy swung by and stood off to the side for a few moments before winking at Millie and continuing toward the theater. The grand prize, a ship on a stick, was awarded to a group of young passengers who managed to answer every single sports question correctly.

Millie handed each of them a plastic "Siren of the Seas" ship on a stick. "I guess I need to ramp up the questions. You guys are good."

After trivia, she headed to the theater to assist Zack, another of the dancers, with several rounds of bingo. The crowd grew and filled the theater. "Must be raining outside," Millie commented, after selling out her first pack of bingo cards.

"Bingo," Zack quipped. "Rain is good for business."

The bingo sessions ended and Millie wandered down to the crew mess to grab a bite to eat. It had been hours since she'd eaten her makeshift breakfast sandwich and soon, she would have to assist Pierre LeBlanc, the sommelier, for the wine tasting event up on deck six.

As Millie ate a bowl of stew, she wondered if Cat had been successful in finding out who bunked with Paloma.

If only she knew.

***

Cat Wellington took a deep breath, lifted her hand and tapped lightly on the outer door of the medical center. The light was on but no one answered so Cat gently twisted the handle, pushed the door open and stepped inside.

There was no one in the front waiting room, but she could hear the clanging of cabinet doors in the back, where the medical equipment and several hospital beds were located. The room reeked of rubbing alcohol and disinfectant.

"Hello?"

The noise stopped and Rachel Quaid appeared in the doorway. "Hi Cat. How're you doing?"

"Okay," Cat said and then quickly realized she needed a reason to visit the medical center. "Actually, I'm feeling a little queasy today. Not sure if I ate a bad batch of something so I wondered if I could get a packet of antacids from you."

"Sure." Rachel smiled. "Be right back."

Cat gazed around the office while she waited for Rachel to return. "Here you go." She dropped the packet in Cat's hand. "I'm sure you heard all about Luigi Falco's unfortunate accident."

"Yes. It would be hard not to." This was too easy! The woman was already talking.

"It sounds like he had his share of enemies, including the higher ups." Rachel made an upward thumbing motion. "Guess I better watch my "p's" and "q's" with a killer on the loose."

"Yes," Cat agreed. "You never can be too careful."

"That girlfriend of his, she must be taking this hard," Rachel continued.

"Paloma," Cat nodded.

"Yes. Paloma Herdez. My guess is she'll be off the ship when we dock in Miami. If I were her, I would head straight home so when the baby comes along, she has family to help her care for it."

Chapter 11

Cat stared at Rachel. "Baby? Paloma is pregnant?"

Rachel's hand flew to her mouth. "Oh my gosh! Did I say that out loud?"

"Yes, you did."

"I...you can't tell anyone you heard it from me," Rachel begged. "I could lose my job."

Cat's window of opportunity flew wide open. "Oh, my lips are sealed Rachel, but I do have a favor to ask. You don't mind, do you? I mean, now that I'm keeping this secret."

Rachel took a step back, a flicker of distrust crossing her face. "What kind of favor?" she asked suspiciously.

"I need two things," Cat rattled off. "First, I need the name of Paloma's cabin mate and two, I need a copy of her work schedule."

"Why?" Rachel asked.

Cat ignored the question. "I'm sure getting your hands on this information would be super easy, one hand tied behind your back, a walk in the park."

Rachel frowned. "Of course I can. In fact, I already have the name of Paloma's cabin mate. It's Hazelle Kahn. She works on the same floor as Paloma up on panorama deck in housekeeping. She cleans the spa suites and the bathrooms outside the pool area. She came in here last week with a bad rash on her..."

"I don't need to hear that part." Cat shuddered. "What does their work schedule look like?"

Rachel shrugged. "It's the same for all of the housekeeping staff. They're on the job by 7:30

a.m. with a break around noon and then back at it in the early evening until late at night."

"Why?" Rachel asked a second time.

"Oh, no reason," Cat shrugged. "Thanks for the info." She reached for the door handle and then turned back. "Your secret is safe with me." She winked at Rachel and hurried out of the door, pulling it shut behind her. "That was a piece of cake."

***

"Pregnant?" Millie gasped as she read the words Cat had scribbled on the sheet of paper. "I. Wow. That's all I can say, other than, poor Paloma."

"Remember, I promised Rachel I wouldn't *say* anything," Cat reminded them. "Your lips are sealed."

Annette drummed her fingers on the counter as she stared at the slip of paper. "I wonder if the baby belongs to Luigi."

115

"Or Carmine," Millie said. "What if it's Carmine's?" The information opened up a whole new can of worms in the investigation.

Cat flipped the sheet of paper over. "We have Carmine as the prime suspect now that we know he had a thing for Paloma, Luigi's girlfriend. We also have Marcus and the other electricians, not to mention Paloma."

"And there's still Captain Armati and Andy who haven't been cleared."

"We need to search Paloma's cabin," Millie said. "Somehow, Luigi's death is tied to Paloma, whether directly or indirectly. We know the captain and Andy didn't take him out but I think the news of the pregnancy triggered something."

"What if Luigi committed suicide?" Cat asked. "I mean, think about it. He had to face his wife and he just found out his girlfriend was pregnant. The day he died, Andy filed a complaint against him so he may have also been facing a job loss."

"It's an interesting angle," Annette admitted. "But why electrocute yourself? Why not just jump overboard or hang yourself?"

"Personally, I don't think Luigi committed suicide. Doesn't fit his personality type," Millie said as she glanced at her watch. "I'm gonna call it a night and be up early to make sure I have enough time to search Paloma's cabin right after her shift starts."

"Better not get caught," Cat fretted.

"I don't plan on it." Millie remembered the time the trio had snuck into Purser Donovan Sweeney's office and gotten caught. Donovan had placed Millie on probation and her master key temporarily taken from her with a warning that if it happened again, she would lose some of her special privileges, including access to the bridge and other restricted areas of the ship.

"I'll let you know if I find anything," Millie said.

Annette gave a small salute. "I think a thorough inspection of the crime scene is in order, although I'm sure Patterson and his men have already searched the area."

Millie followed Cat to the gift shop and inside where she fired up the ship's computer and cash register so they could figure out which cabin belonged to Paloma and her cabin mate, Hazelle.

All ship employees were assigned a bar account, an account that enabled them to purchase store items, beverages on board, salon services and even buy internet minutes. The crewmembers were required to settle the account at the end of each month and the online system linked the employee name and account number to their cabin.

Cat frowned as she waited for the screen to pop up. "You don't think I could get in trouble for giving you this information?"

"Nah!" Millie waved a hand. "I could log into the system myself and get it, if I knew where to look. Don't worry, if I get busted, I won't throw you under the bus." She patted Cat's arm.

Cat tapped the keyboard as she typed Paloma's name. Moments later, a screen popped up, listing the woman's account number and cabin number. Cat reached for a pen and jotted the number on the sheet of paper, right next to the list of suspects. She folded the sheet in half and handed it to Millie. "Do not lose this."

"I won't." Millie promised as she slipped the note into her pocket. "Thanks for the information."

Cat followed Millie out of the store, turned the lights off and locked the door behind her. "I've been thinking about the woman, you know the psycho – whatever."

"And?" Millie stopped abruptly and studied her friend's face.

"I'm willing to talk to her when we reach St. Thomas." Cat looked around and lowered her voice. "Please don't tell anyone."

"My lips are sealed." Millie made a zipping motion across her lips and then impulsively hugged her friend. "I'm glad Cat. This is a good thing and if you want, I'll be right there with you," she promised.

Millie headed down to her cabin. She wondered if perhaps she should steer clear of the investigation and let Patterson and his men handle it.

She decided to sleep on it, if you could call it that since she tossed and turned all night, wondering why Captain Armati was transferring to another ship and why he still hadn't deemed it important enough to discuss it with her.

Millie was hurt that she had to find out from someone else that he was leaving Siren of the Seas. Had he not thought enough of their relationship to tell her in person? She had a feeling he planned to tell her the other day in his apartment.

It was almost as if he was avoiding her and before she finally drifted off to sleep in the early hours of the morning, she decided to leave the ball in his court.

Danielle snuck into the cabin at some point during the night. Millie didn't bother checking the clock and assumed her young cabin mate had been hanging out with some of her friends down in the employee lounge.

Millie didn't know what to think of the new employee, Lorenzo. There was something about him that didn't ring true, although she couldn't quite put her finger on it.

She made a mental note to broach the subject with Danielle before, once again, falling into a fitful sleep.

When her alarm blared in the wee hours of the morning, Millie quickly shut it off before she crept out of bed and made her way to the bathroom.

Millie hoped the alarm hadn't woken Danielle, who would be curious as to why Millie was up so early.

She had set the alarm for 6:30, which would give her plenty of time to grab a light breakfast in the crew mess before heading to the other end of the ship where the housekeeping staffs' cabins were located.

The ship shuddered several times while Millie dressed, which meant they had docked in St. Thomas. Today was going to be a busy one, between snooping around inside Paloma's cabin, to seeing passengers off the ship for a day ashore, not to mention tracking down Dr. Johansen to see if she could meet with Cat.

Millie had tucked her work clothes in the back of one of the bathroom shelves the night before so she wouldn't have to rummage around the cabin in the dark.

When she finished getting ready, she flipped the bathroom light off and slowly turned the door handle, stepping into the small cabin and coming face-to-face with a wide awake and fully-dressed Danielle. "Where are you off to so bright and early this fine morning?"

"Breakfast," Millie said, which was true. She had enough time to grab a quick breakfast before the housekeeping staff headed upstairs to start their day.

"Huh." Danielle didn't buy it for a second. "Then what?"

"Just checking out a few leads in Luigi's murder investigation," she answered vaguely.

"Aha!" Danielle hopped out of the chair. "I knew it." She rubbed her hands together. "I want to help. What are we going to do? Set up surveillance? A sting?"

"Neither. I'm going to take a quick peek inside Paloma Herdez's cabin."

"How are you going to do that? Knock on her cabin door and tell her you'd like to take a look around because you think she murdered her lover?"

"No." Millie lowered her gaze. "Not exactly."

"Ah!" Danielle gasped. "You're going to break into her cabin?"

"Break is a strong word," Millie said. "More like let myself in for a quick look around."

Danielle shrugged. "Break. Snoop. Same thing. I want to go with you."

"This is kind of a one man...er, woman operation." Visions of Danielle fumbling around and causing them to be caught popped into her head. There were times Danielle was like a bull in a china shop. Act first, think later.

"C'mon, Millie," Danielle pleaded. "Andy is my boss, too."

Millie wrinkled her nose. She did not want Danielle tagging along but somehow, she had a feeling if she didn't take her with, she'd end up involved, somehow, and probably not in a good way.

"Okay," Millie caved. "But you have to be stealth. We need to be quick, quiet and invisible."

"Got it." Danielle gave her the thumbs up and hurried to the bathroom. "Give me a minute and I'll be ready to go." She swung the door open and disappeared inside.

Danielle began to hum loudly.

Millie stared at the bathroom door and shook her head. "What have I gotten myself into?"

Chapter 12

Millie's armpits grew damp as she cast a furtive glance down the long hall and lifted her lanyard from around her neck. Her hand trembled as she slipped her keycard into Paloma's cabin door. The lock clicked. Millie twisted the handle and then eased the door open. "Hello? Anybody home?"

Danielle, who was right behind Millie, nudged her forward, stepping on the back of her heel as she pushed her inside.

"Ouch!" Millie gasped.

"Sorry. Keep moving." Danielle waved her hands, motioning Millie into the dark cabin. "Before someone spots us."

The door quietly closed behind them and they stood motionless in the dark. "Don't we need to turn the light on to see inside?" Danielle whispered.

"Maybe we shouldn't do this," Millie said as she began having second thoughts.

"It's a little late now," Danielle hissed.

"I guess you're right. Let me try to find the light switch." Millie hoped the layout of Paloma and Hazelle's cabin was the same as theirs. Danielle had been in such a hurry to close the door; she hadn't had time to scope it out.

She ran her hand along the side of the wall. "Closet. Their layout is flip-flopped." It meant the light switch was on the opposite wall. Millie slid her hand along the wall before making contact with the switch. She flipped the switch on and bright light flooded the small cabin.

"Holy smokes." Danielle's mouth dropped open as she stared at the cabin. "It looks like a tornado touched down!"

Discarded clothes covered every square inch of the floor. Dirty dishes teetered precariously on top of the small desk. Propped in the corner of the room was a foot tall stack of plastic drink glasses.

"That smell," Danielle muttered under her breath. "It smells like..."

"A locker room," Millie suggested.

"Yeah, or a garbage dump," Danielle said. "Gross." She swatted at a small gnat that buzzed around her head. "Let's hurry and get this over with before we get cooties or something."

Millie grinned. "You're the one who wanted to tag along."

Danielle ignored the jab and reached past Millie to open the top desk drawer. She flipped several sheets of paper over and glanced at the front before deeming them junk. There were also several ink pens, a few loose paperclips and a book of stamps.

She opened the next drawer, which was full of hairbands, bobby pins, barrettes and a piece of purple metallic material. Danielle wrinkled her nose and held it out for inspection. "What is this?"

Millie, who had been digging around the center desk drawer, looked up. "I can't say for certain because I've never worn one, but it looks like string bikini underwear."

Danielle dropped the underwear and rubbed her hand on the front of her slacks. "We should've brought rubber gloves!"

"True." Millie hadn't thought of that. She turned her attention to the drawer, which contained a writing tablet, a locked journal, some gel pens and a cell phone.

"Jackpot!" Millie grabbed the phone and pressed the side button. Nothing happened. "How do I turn this phone on?"

Danielle snatched the cell phone from Millie and pressed several buttons on the screen. "There are some pictures on here." The women huddled over the phone, peering at the screen.

The first few pictures were of Paloma and Hazelle inside their cabin. There were other pictures that included waterfalls, smiling passengers standing in front of their cabins, as well as pictures of other crewmembers.

"Wait!" Millie caught a glimpse of a young, dark-haired woman, her arms wrapped around another crewmember. "Go back."

Danielle slid her finger across the screen.

"There."

Danielle tapped the screen and enlarged the picture. At first glance, it looked like a photo of Paloma and Marcus, the electrical engineer, locked in a tight embrace.

Millie pointed at the screen. "That's Marcus. He worked under Luigi."

"And Carmine," Danielle said.

The door handle began to rattle.

"Someone's coming!" Millie dropped the phone and quickly eased the drawer shut as her eyes darted frantically around the small cabin. "In here!"

Danielle flipped the light switch off. The women dashed into the small bathroom, closing the door behind them.

Millie squeezed her eyes shut and held her breath, praying whoever had entered the cabin would not open the bathroom door. She could hear someone mumbling on the other side of the door and then a couple muffled thuds before another, louder thud.

"I think they're gone," Danielle whispered.

"Let's wait another minute." Millie's heart began to pound as she stood in the small, cramped dark space. Her claustrophobia began to kick in. When she couldn't stand it a second longer, she swung the door open and peeked out.

The room was dark. "They're gone."

Danielle flipped the light switch back on. "We need a picture of the picture."

"Good idea." Millie pulled the cellphone from the drawer and handed it to Danielle who quickly flipped it on and thumbed through the photos. When she got to the one of the cozy couple, she set it on the desk, reached in her back pocket, pulled her own cell phone out, switched it to on and began snapping photos.

They thumbed through a few more photos before Millie decided it was time to wrap up their covert operation. "We need to take a quick look through here and then get out before we get caught."

Danielle quickly searched the bunkbeds while Millie finished checking the drawers and then moved onto the closets. She opened one of the doors and peered inside. It was stacked floor to ceiling with dirty clothes.

The stench of dirty laundry and sweat was overpowering and she began to gag. Millie quickly shut the door. "No way am I touching that mess."

Danielle had moved onto the bathroom for a quick search while Millie checked the other closet, which was in the same deplorable condition.

There was only one thing left to inspect...the garbage. Millie picked up the overflowing trashcan and, using the tip of her index finger, shifted a few items to the side. The pungent smell of rotting fruit wafted up.

Danielle burst out of the bathroom. "Disgusting. I don't know how someone could expect to come out of that bathroom cleaner than when they went in."

Millie set the trashcan down and stuck her hands on her hips. "I think I've seen enough."

"I *know* I've seen enough, and smelled enough," Danielle said. "Let's get out of here." They started to head toward the door when something caught Millie's eye. It was a piece of paper, barely visible, tucked behind the vanity mirror that hung over the desk.

Millie pinched the corner between her fingers and tugged until she had pulled the paper, which she now realized was an envelope, from its hiding spot. She flipped it over:

Maria Falco

West Seaside Lane 10855

13329 Cochem

Germany

Chapter 13

It was a small envelope and, judging by the thickness and weight, Millie guessed it contained a single sheet of paper.

Danielle, who had been standing near the exit with one hand on the door handle, strode across the small cabin and stared at the envelope, reading the words neatly printed on the front. "Luigi's wife."

"I'd bet a million bucks." Millie stared at the addressed envelope. "I wonder when Paloma wrote this."

"Before Luigi died? Maybe Paloma was going to tell Luigi's wife about their relationship."

"Or the baby," Millie added.

"Baby?" Danielle's eyes widened. "Are you saying Paloma is pregnant?"

The words had slipped out of Millie's mouth without her thinking about what she'd said. "Did I say baby? I meant rabies."

"No you didn't," Danielle argued. "I heard you. You said baby."

"You're right." Millie placed the envelope behind the mirror, right where she'd found it. "You can't breathe a word to anyone, Danielle. I'm not supposed to know and neither are you."

"Did Paloma tell you she was pregnant? I didn't know you knew her."

"I don't. Let's discuss this somewhere else. The longer we stand here, the greater our risk of being caught."

The women hurried out of the cabin. Millie flipped the lights off while Danielle eased the door open and peeked around the corner. "The coast is clear."

The women stepped into the corridor and Millie let the door close behind them before glancing at her watch: 7:45. They had only been inside the cabin ten minutes and in that time had managed to find two clues. The cell phone picture and the letter addressed to a person Millie was convinced was Luigi's wife.

It didn't make Paloma a killer, nor did it make Marcus a killer, but it moved them both up a notch on the list of suspects, along with Carmine, who had been, and was, Luigi and Marcus's boss. There were three strong suspects, all with motive. Paloma, a possibly spurned and pregnant lover. Marcus, who may have been in love with Paloma and when he found out she was pregnant with Luigi's baby, he killed him in a fit of anger.

What if Paloma, looking to move up the ranks, began dating Carmine? Somehow, Luigi found out about the relationship and/or the baby. The more Millie uncovered, the more convinced she was that Paloma held the key.

The fact Luigi had died by electrocution bumped Carmine and Marcus to the top of the list with Paloma underneath. Paloma probably wouldn't have the knowledge to know how to electrocute her lover.

Millie shuddered. It was a horrible way to die, not that there was a good way to die. She offered a small prayer for Luigi and his family as she and Danielle wandered back to their cabin in silence.

Millie waited while Danielle unlocked their door and stepped inside. She dropped her lanyard on the desktop. "I feel dirty, just being inside their cabin. Aren't cleaning people supposed to be clean?"

"You know the saying," Millie said, "a mechanic's car is always broken. A plumber's sink always leaks. The last thing those women want to do when they finish working 12-hour days is to clean their cabin."

"True. I'm going to scrub my hands." Danielle disappeared inside their bathroom as Millie glanced around. Perhaps Danielle wasn't such a bad cabin mate after all. For the most part, she was tidy and respectful of coming in quietly after hours.

She wondered if Danielle was still hot after the new employee, Lorenzo.

Danielle emerged from the bathroom a short time later. "I feel much better."

"How's Lorenzo?"

"Lorenzo?" Danielle stood in front of the full-length mirror and combed her long blonde locks with her fingers.

"Lorenzo. Your new love interest. The hottie who started working in housekeeping."

"Oh, that Lorenzo." Danielle shrugged nonchalantly. "He's okay. I've only met up with him a couple times down in the employee lounge. He works a lot of hours."

"Huh." Millie nodded and then stood. "Speaking of work, we need to start our day." For the second time, she nearly slipped up with Danielle and mentioned she needed to contact Dr. Rebecca Johansen to see if she could meet Cat on board the ship.

"You're doing your usual greet and go?" Danielle asked.

"Yep. Speaking of which, I have ten minutes to make it to the gangway before Andy starts blowing up my radio."

The women departed their cabin and went their separate ways. Millie wasn't sure what Andy had put on Danielle's plate but he typically liked to keep her busy with the ship's junior passengers, entertaining the handful who didn't go ashore with their families.

Millie had always said she'd love to dabble in the kids programs, but all of the other activities Andy filled her day with left little room to branch out and try working in new areas, not that she minded. Millie loved the variety of activities...the wine tasting with Pierre, bingo with Zack, trivia, not to mention the line dancing and polka with the dancers, Alison and Tara.

Andy was standing near the gangway when Millie arrived. He glanced at his watch. "You're right on time."

"Of course. Have I ever let you down?" she joked.

Millie held up her hand. "Don't answer that."

A couple with two young children approached, asking what time they should be back on board the ship before heading ashore.

The next two hours flew by. St. Thomas was one of the more popular cruise ports, and included Magens Bay, once voted one of the most beautiful beaches on the planet.

Captain Armati had mentioned perhaps snorkeling or kayaking in Magens Bay, but it looked like that was never going to happen.

Millie's heart plummeted and she quickly shoved the thought out of her head. She couldn't dwell on it, not now. Maybe not ever.

After the crowds thinned, Andy told Millie she was free for the next few hours. "I'm going ashore," Millie announced.

"Shopping?" Andy asked. St. Thomas was wildly popular for not only the island's beautiful beaches but for amazing deals on jewelry. There was a large shopping area just outside the docking area, with tons of souvenir shops and jewelry stores, not to mention restaurants and bars.

Passengers and crew could hang out right there. For the passengers on board, looking to get a great deal on unique jewelry and large gems, St. Thomas was the place to go.

Millie had gone ashore on a previous stop, but she had such a small amount of storage space in the shared cabin, she only purchased the necessities, which meant a quick trip to the drugstore, located inside the shopping area.

"No. I have an errand to run." Millie left it at that. She didn't want to broadcast Cat's potential meeting with the psychologist, although she knew Andy wouldn't say anything. Still, it felt more like gossip so she decided the less said the better.

She'd already done enough damage earlier when she spilled the beans to Danielle about Paloma's pregnancy.

Andy glanced at his watch. "Remember to be back on board by 2:30 so we can start greeting guests around three o'clock."

Millie promised she would before making her way off the ship. She'd already packed a backpack with her cell phone, her wallet, a bottled water and an umbrella in case the heat became unbearable.

She cleared the ship area and the shopping area and wandered down the sidewalk to a small park bench, shaded by a cluster of tall trees. It took a few minutes for Millie's cell phone to boot up and she waited for a signal. When she finally had decent reception, she noticed she had a new voicemail message.

It was Dr. Johansen, who told Millie she saved a spot in her schedule for eleven a.m., but told her to call as soon as the ship docked because she might be able to come earlier.

Cat was off work for most of the day since the ship's gift shop closed while the ship was in port. Millie had checked with her before disembarking and Cat promised to leave her cell phone on so that Millie could contact her if she was able to reach the doctor and bring her on board.

She'd also filled Annette in on the progress and, unfortunately, Annette was scheduled to work all day so Millie was on her own. She dialed the doctor's number and left a message.

Millie disconnected the line and plopped down on the park bench. There was a small coffee shop, directly across the street. With time to spare, she grabbed her backpack, crossed the busy street and wandered inside.

The smell of freshly roasted coffee and cinnamon filled the air. She sniffed appreciatively and eyed the cinnamon rolls, raspberry twists and chocolate covered donuts arranged on the wire racks inside the display case.

She walked over to the counter and gazed at the chalkboard menu overhead. "I'll have a French vanilla swirl iced coffee and a chocolate covered donut."

Millie reached inside her backpack and pulled out a five-dollar bill plus a couple ones.

"That'll be $9.15."

Millie's mouth dropped open. "Nine dollars and fifteen cents for an iced coffee and a chocolate donut?"

"Yes ma'am."

Millie pulled out a ten instead, and told the girl to keep the change, vowing to buy her coffee and treats on board the ship from now on. She'd always thought the coffee shop was on the pricey side but this place had them beat.

She adjusted her backpack and then picked up the donut and coffee. Millie carefully carried the liquid gold and overpriced donut out of the coffee shop before easing onto a small bench out front. She nibbled on her treat as she watched traffic and passengers pass by. As she sipped her coffee, she thought about poor Paloma, pregnant and thousands of miles away from family and friends.

Had Luigi said something that sent Paloma over the edge, causing her to commit a crime of passion? Perhaps it was someone else, bent on revenge.

Millie's cell phone beeped and she carefully juggled her coffee in one hand and cell phone in the other as she gazed at the screen. It was Captain Armati. He'd sent a text, asking her to please stop by the bridge when she had time.

She clicked out of the text without replying, still hurt by the fact he hadn't bothered to explain to her why, exactly, he was transferring to another ship and why she was the last to know.

Millie took a big bite of the donut. The thick layer of creamy chocolate melted in her mouth and she decided the donut was worth every penny. Chocolate therapy. She polished off the sweet treat and washed it down with a big swig of iced coffee.

There was another message Millie had missed. It was her daughter, Beth. Beth and Millie's son, Blake, both had their mother's ship schedule and Millie called Beth once a week while in port.

Millie quickly dialed her daughter's number and a breathless Beth picked up on the first ring. "Hi Mom."

"Hi Beth. You sound out of breath."

"Yeah," her daughter groaned. "Noah caught some sort of bug and we just got back from the doctor." Noah was Millie's grandson.

"I hope he's going to be okay."

"He'll be fine," Beth said. "Last night David and I were discussing the fact we're long overdue for a vacation."

Millie's heart skipped a beat. "Tell me you've decided to come on a cruise."

"Yep," her daughter confirmed. "But it won't be until after the school year ends."

"I think I'll have my break before then." Millie knew she was getting close to the end of her contract. She wondered if Majestic Cruise Lines would ask her to come back.

"We can't wait to see you," Beth said. Mother and daughter talked for several long minutes, until Beth told her Noah was hollering for his mother.

A wave of sadness washed over Millie as she thought about how much she missed her children and grandchildren. She reminded herself she would see them soon and then reached for her phone to place a second call to Doctor Johansen when it began to ring. It was the doctor. "Hello?"

"Is this Millie Sanders?" a woman asked in a clipped tone.

"Yes, this is Millie."

"Hi Millie. Doctor Johansen here. I'm in my car, driving to the port and wondered where you would like to meet."

Millie told her to make her way to the security gate and that she would meet her there.

Dave Patterson's department had ramped up security after a recent hijacking incident. It was possible security would need to call the bridge to verify the woman's clearance.

Millie chugged the rest of her chilled caffeine before tossing the empty cup into the trash along with the donut wrapper and paper napkin. She hurried across the street and power-walked to the shopping area. She didn't slow her pace until she reached the gate.

Standing near the gate was a woman with short blonde hair. She was tall and thin, and staring at her watch.

"Dr. Johansen?"

The woman looked up, her gray eyes meeting Millie's eyes. "Yes?"

Millie extended her hand. "I'm Millie Sanders, Assistant Cruise Director aboard Siren of the Seas. Thank you for meeting me here."

Millie turned to the security guards standing next to the gate. She recognized one as Carlos, the ship's security and another uniformed man Millie guessed was a St. Thomas port security personnel. "Dr. Johansen has clearance from Captain Armati to board Siren of the Seas for a couple hours."

Carlos pulled a clipboard from a small table nearby and flipped through the sheets, running his finger down the column. "Yes, I see Miss Millie." He turned to the doctor. "I'll need to see a photo ID."

Dr. Johansen fumbled inside her purse, pulled out her wallet and flipped it open. She turned it and Carlos studied the picture. "Thank you." He waved them through. "You'll escort Dr. Johansen off the ship when finished?"

"Of course." Millie smiled and then waited for Dr. Johansen to drop her wallet back inside her purse. During their stroll, Millie briefly reiterated her reason for asking Dr. Johansen to chat with Cat. During the short conversation, Millie determined she liked the doctor's demeanor. She seemed calm, thoughtful and reserved.

They stopped just before crossing over the gangway and entering the ship. "My fee for today's session is one hundred twenty-five dollars for an hour. The price includes an out-of-office visit."

"Of course. Millie had already gotten the price via the doctor's website. Annette and Millie had split the cost, each contributing half. She pulled the bills from her small wallet inside her backpack, counted out the money and handed it to the woman, who folded the cash and stuffed it into the side of her purse.

When they reached the inside of the ship, Millie led Dr. Johansen one deck up, the deck where crew quarters and Cat's cabin were located.

She had texted Annette on her way back to the ship and Annette had said she would meet her at the end of the corridor before they introduced Cat to the doctor.

When they got to the corridor, Annette was already outside, pacing. She stopped when Millie and Dr. Johansen approached. "I was lucky I was able to break away. Amit nearly set the kitchen on fire this morning. He was experimenting on a dish of cherries jubilee and added too much brandy. Then he attempted to light it with a mini torch, the ones we use for baked Alaska."

Annette flung her hands in the air. "Poof!" She grabbed a chunk of hair. "I didn't have time to look. Did he singe my bangs or eyebrows? I smell a burnt odor."

Millie leaned forward and inspected Annette's hair and eyebrows. "I don't see anything."

"Good." Annette rolled her eyes. "Made me want to grab that bottle of brandy and chugalug. Only Amit can drive me to drink."

Dr. Johansen interrupted. "How long have you been experiencing these feelings of...anger and frustration that makes you want to drink to drown your sorrows?"

Millie dissolved into a fit of laughter and clutched her stomach. "No! I'm sorry Doctor Johansen. You're here to see Cat. She's the one who is experiencing fears and anxiety."

She pointed to Annette. "This is our mutual friend, Annette."

Dr. Johansen tilted her head and studied Annette. "I still see signs of regressive behavior you might want to address."

Annette frowned at the doctor while Millie swiped at the tears rolling down her cheeks. "Cat's cabin is this way."

When they reached Cat's cabin, Millie lightly tapped on the door. "Cat. It's me, Millie."

No one answered so Millie knocked again, this time harder. There was still no answer. "Let me try her cell phone." Millie fumbled in her backpack, pulled out her cellphone and dialed Cat's number. It went to voice mail. She turned to Annette. "Now what?"

Chapter 14

Millie hoped Cat hadn't intentionally changed her mind and was avoiding the doctor.

"We can try to track her down," Annette said. "I'll run by the gift shop to see if she's hiding out there or better yet, you can use your key to get inside to see if she's hiding in the back room."

Millie shook her head. "Unfortunately, my master key doesn't work in the gift shops. The shops are run by independent third parties and have nothing to do with the cruise line."

Disappointed, the trio turned to go. They made it halfway down the hall when they ran into Cat, who was hurrying toward them. "I'm sorry," she said breathlessly. "Donovan Sweeney called me to his office and I just left."

"We thought you bailed on us," Annette said.

Millie turned to Dr. Johansen. "Dr. Johansen, this is Cat Wellington." The women shook hands and Cat led them back down the hall before opening her cabin door.

"I'll return in forty minutes to walk Dr. Johansen off the ship," Millie told Cat and the doctor before the door shut behind them. She turned to Annette. "Regressive behavior," she chuckled.

"That's absurd," Annette sputtered. "I'm one of the most well-adjusted individuals I know."

Millie was still chuckling when they parted ways near the steps leading to the upper decks. She had decided to hang out in her cabin, not far from Cat's, in case something came up and Cat needed her.

She strode down the hall and spied someone in an officer's uniform standing at the other end of the corridor. As she drew closer, Millie realized it was Captain Armati.

She slowed her steps and stopped in front of the door.

"You've been avoiding me," the captain said.

"I've been busy," Millie replied. "I'm sure you have been busy, too...busy packing."

"Can we discuss this privately?" Captain Armati's eyes met Millie's eyes. He owed her an explanation and although her pride wanted to tell him not to bother, the other part of her, her heart, told her to give him a chance to explain.

"Yes." She slipped her keycard in the slot and then pushed the door open. "What if someone sees you follow me into my cabin?"

Captain Armati slowly smiled. "Millie, everyone on board the ship knows we're an item. We're old news."

"True." She held the door and waited for him to step inside before closing the door behind him.

He gazed around the cramped space. "I forgot how small these crew quarters were."

Millie tossed her lanyard on the desk. "I don't spend a lot of time here, except to sleep and shower, although there are times it seems somewhat claustrophobic, especially when Danielle and I are both in here."

"Ah, Danielle."

Captain Armati eased into the small desk chair and Millie sat on the edge of her bunk, staring at him expectantly.

The captain clasped his hands and lowered his gaze, as if searching for the right words. "I'm sorry I didn't tell you of the ship transfer earlier. I was hoping something would happen and I wouldn't have to leave."

"But you are, aren't you?" she asked.

Their eyes met and he slowly nodded. "I am. I have one more week and then Scout and I move to Baroness of the Seas." He continued. "I didn't

159

feel I had a choice. There's a reason I requested the transfer but I can't discuss it right now."

Captain Armati shifted in the chair. "I should have known better than to have started our relationship. I was being selfish. It's just that I've never met anyone like you. You have spunk, you're caring, you're funny. Millie, you're the whole package and I couldn't resist."

She heard the words but all she could think was that it was over. He was moving on and leaving her behind. The feelings of rejection she'd experienced when Roger had left her for Delilah Osborne came flooding back.

Her lower lip started to tremble and she clenched her jaw in an attempt to control her emotions.

Millie Sanders would survive. This was nothing compared to having her spouse walk out after 38 years of marriage. "I appreciate your kind words. You're a wonderful man and I guess

I let myself get caught up in a shipboard romance."

The captain cut her off. "It was more than a shipboard romance," he said. "At least it was for me."

There wasn't much else to say and Millie stood.

Captain Armati studied her for a moment before standing and making his way to the door. "I'm sorry."

"Me too." Millie trailed behind and stopped in front of the cabin door. She turned the handle and pulled the door open. "I appreciate the fact you came by to explain."

The captain sucked in a breath, as if ready to say something else, but instead nodded. "You're welcome." He stepped out into the hall and Millie closed the door behind him before she placed her cheek against the cool metal and burst into tears.

***

Millie sobbed her heart out, until there were no more tears left to cry. She shuffled to the bathroom and took a long, hard look at her reflection in the mirror. The sorrow-filled face that stared back made her want to start crying again.

Millie Sanders, you're tougher than that! She scolded as she leaned over the sink, splashing cold water on her hot face. She grabbed her foundation and carefully covered the red splotches on her cheeks and nose with an extra layer of makeup.

She had enough time to head to Cat's cabin to meet Dr. Johansen to accompany her out. The doctor didn't emerge for a full five minutes past the agreed time, but when she did, Cat was with her and her eyes were as red as Millie's eyes had been.

"I'll see you next week, Cat," the doctor said. "Remember, the name of the place is Fabulous

Brew Coffee Shop. Walk past the gate, veer to the right and head up the steps."

"Yes. I'll be there at 11:00, exactly one week from today." Cat solemnly nodded her head.

The doctor turned to Millie. "I'm ready."

The women walked in silence. Millie was dying to ask questions, but the fact Cat had told the doctor she would meet her in a coffee shop off the ship meant she'd made some progress.

Millie accompanied her to the gate and then stopped. "Thank you for fitting us in. I'm sure you can't discuss your patient's status but the fact Cat has agreed to get off the ship next week is a huge step for her."

The doctor nodded and then tilted her head as she studied Millie. "Is everything okay?"

"No," Millie admitted. She gave the doctor a watery smile. "I just got some bad news but this too shall pass." She changed the subject. "Thank you again. I'm not sure if I'll see you next week. It depends on whether Cat needs moral support."

Millie waited for Doctor Johansen to exit through the security gate before turning on her heel and slowly walking back to the ship. She still had several hours before it was time to return to work. On any other day, she would have loved to explore the island.

Now all she wanted to do was go back to her cabin, crawl into bed and cover her head. Instead, Millie made her way to the Sky Chapel.

It was dark and quiet inside. She tiptoed to the front of the chapel, eased into a pew and closed her eyes.

The gnawing anguish in the pit of her stomach made Millie want to throw up. Captain Armati and she had grown close, spending at least one night a week together having dinner or, when they were in port, exploring one of the islands or trying a new dish at one of the island restaurants.

Millie thought about Scout. She would miss him when he was gone. A small tear escaped and trickled down her cheek unchecked. Life could be so cruel. The thought crossed her mind that maybe she wouldn't renew her contract. Maybe it was time to go home.

Her contract was ending soon and it would be time to head home for her break. She missed her children, missed the small town feel of Grand Rapids. Occasionally, but not often, she even missed the changing seasons.

"Hello Millie."

Millie shifted in the pew and watched as Pastor Pete Evans, the ship's clergy, ambled down the aisle. He squeezed past Millie and then eased onto the pew next to her.

She quickly swiped at her tear-stained cheeks but it was too late. He shifted his gaze and stared at the cross, front and center.

"Be joyful in hope, patient in affliction, faithful in prayer. Romans 12: 12." (NIV) "That is my verse for today, Millie," Pastor Evans said. "It was in my devotional and I've been meditating on it all morning."

"I needed to hear that," Millie whispered as she lowered her head and studied her hands. "I'm not having a good day."

Pastor Evans patted her arm. "We'll all miss Captain Armati and Scout, but no one more than you, I'm sure."

Millie could only nod as the lump in her throat swelled. They sat quietly for several long moments as Millie focused on her many blessings...her health, her friends, her children and grandchildren, not to mention a job she loved.

Pastor Evans broke the silence as he made small talk about the weather before easing off the bench. "I'll leave you alone with God. Trust in Him Millie. All the rest will fall into place."

"I know." Millie released a shaky breath. "I just gotta let that sink in."

Pastor Evans' footsteps echoed on the tile floor as he exited the sanctuary.

Millie sat motionless for several long moments, in deep conversation with her Creator before sliding off the bench and shuffling out of the chapel.

Chapter 15

"You're going to run the Killer Karaoke again tonight." Andy didn't pose it as a question to Millie, but rather a statement.

The busier the better was Millie's new motto. She needed to push through her slump and lingering feelings of sadness. The best way to do that was stay so busy, she had no time to dwell on anything else. "Of course," she nodded.

They were standing near the gangway, waiting for the passengers to board. It was t-minus ten minutes and counting. Oscar had stopped by to let them know an entire busload of passengers, who had gone on a zip-lining excursion early that morning, hadn't returned. It was a ship-sponsored excursion, which meant the cruise ship would wait for the passengers to return.

According to Oscar, the bus was stuck in a traffic jam and at least half an hour out. Time was money for cruise lines. The port charged the cruise line for every minute they remained docked past their scheduled departure. She had no idea what the charge would be and probably didn't want to know.

The last stragglers returning to the ship trickled to nothing and the six o'clock departure passed. Finally, at 6:20, a group of harried passengers darted up the gangway, dinging their keycards in the machine as they boarded.

"Welcome back. Glad you could join us," Andy joked.

Some of the guest grinned, while others looked frazzled.

"Everyone is back on board," Suharto, the security guard manning the entrance, announced after a couple, dragging two teenage boys, brought up the rear.

The crew quickly removed the gangway, closed the door and moments later the ship began to shudder as it pulled away from the dock.

Millie glanced at her watch. "I'm going to grab a quick burger and then head upstairs to check on the poolside party." The poolside party was the current day's version of the sail away party.

The place was packed and Millie spotted Danielle up on the large, center stage, supervising the belly flop contest. The sound of steel drums filled the air and clusters of passengers lounged near the pool while others sat at nearby tables, munching on pre-dinner snacks.

Millie quickly filled her plate with a hamburger, a piece of lettuce, sliced tomatoes and onion, along with a mound of crispy French fries. There was even a small spot left on her plate for a crispy chicken tender.

Millie carried her plate and glass of iced tea to the quietest corner she could find.

Danielle, who finished hosting the belly flop contest, wandered over. "I didn't know they were serving chicken tenders today. Be right back." She darted down the steps, returning a short time later with a plateful of chicken tenders. She eased into the seat next to Millie and then reached for a tender on top. "Have you made any progress on the investigation today?"

"Nope." Millie assembled her burger, squirted some mayonnaise and mustard on top of the patty before popping the bun on top of the burger and taking a big bite. She was hungrier than she realized and waited to finish chewing her food before answering. "I've had my hands full. I'm sure you heard all about the late departure."

"Yep." Danielle rolled her eyes. "One of the passengers near the hurricane bar on deck twelve had a major meltdown. Seems she let two of her teenagers take the zip lining excursion without a parental unit accompanying them and she was freaking out that they weren't back."

"I would've too. Can you imagine the ship sailing away, knowing your children were on an island in the middle of the ocean?"

Danielle dipped her chicken tender into the honey mustard sauce and bit the end. "Have you checked out the scene of the crime?"

"Nope. It's on my list."

"How about going now? We can run down there after we eat," Danielle said.

Millie planned to check it out with Annette, not Danielle, but once again, the young woman managed to plant herself firmly in the middle of one of Millie's investigations. She remembered the time the cruise ship had been hijacked and how Danielle had decided to scale the side of the ship, right in front of the bridge, in an attempt to spy on the ship's hijackers, who were holed up inside.

Danielle's plan had backfired and she ended up falling into the ocean, right before the hijackers began shooting at her.

Danielle had survived the exploit unscathed with the exception of being a little stiff and sore. She was lucky she hadn't been knocked unconscious from the impact of the fall and then drowned.

"Annette and I planned to head down there, but you're welcome to tag along," Millie said. There was no way to stop Danielle and Millie decided it was better to keep an eye on her rather than to let her try to take matters into her own hands.

"Great." Danielle popped the rest of the chicken tender in her mouth. "We'll swing by the galley and pick her up on our way there."

***

Danielle stood guard to make sure no one was coming while Annette and Millie peered at the jumble of melted wire and the charred panel cover.

Annette tugged on the blackened latch that secured the electrical panel. "This is a burned out mess."

The lingering smell of melted plastic and chemical wafted from the box. "I could be staring right at a clue and have no idea what I'm looking at," Millie admitted. "I don't know the first thing about electrical fires."

"I have a little electrical knowledge," Danielle said. "Hazards of a previous job."

"Let's trade places." Annette headed to the corridor to keep watch while Danielle made her way over to the panel. She studied the jumbled mess.

"Andy said he heard a noise and ran out to find Luigi on the floor," Danielle said.

"Yes. He heard a noise," Millie confirmed.

"Which means Luigi could have been electrocuted by an arc flash where the volt travels through the air, electrocuting him."

She went on. "For an arc flash, there has to be some sort of trigger...dust, water or even oil." Danielle tucked her hands behind her back and leaned forward, her eyes narrowing. "See that streak right there?" She nodded her head at the panel door and a dark line. "It looks like oil, which would conduct electricity, causing it to arc."

She straightened. "Someone who knew what they were doing could've sprayed or dribbled oil inside this panel. They called the electrical department...Luigi...to come check it out. Luigi would've opened the door." Danielle snapped her fingers. "Voila. The panel created an arc flash, followed by a sudden bright blinding light and then the explosion."

"But someone would've had to have known what they were doing," Millie said. "Plus, I'm sure Luigi Falco would have turned the breaker off before opening the box."

"True," Danielle said. "Electricity is dangerous stuff and nothing to mess with. Whoever set Luigi up was playing with electricity and could easily have gotten themselves electrocuted."

"Unless they knew what they were doing," Millie repeated.

"Someone's coming," Annette hissed.

Millie, using the tip of her walkie-talkie antenna, quickly closed the panel door. The trio ducked under the rope that secured the area and then hurried inside the theater. They shuffled off to one side and into the shadows.

Andy strolled by and Millie pressed her body flat against the side of the wall.

He must have sensed their presence and abruptly stopped in his tracks. "Millie?"

Chapter 16

Millie relaxed her stance and stepped out of the shadows. "I swear you have eyes in the back of your head."

"What are you..." Andy caught a glimpse of the other women. "That's a silly question. You were snooping around," he said.

"Guilty as charged," Danielle admitted.

"You were investigating the crime scene," he said. "Don't you know how much hot water you'd be in if Patterson caught you?"

"We're only trying to help," Millie said.

"I appreciate that," Andy said, "but getting yourselves killed is only going to make matters worse. What if you were messing around near the panel and one of you got electrocuted?" Andy asked.

Millie hadn't thought about that. Surely, there was no juice flowing to the burned out panel. Andy's statement made Millie feel foolish for dragging her friends into the investigation.

"Danielle thinks someone with electrical knowledge set Luigi up," Annette said.

"The Jill of all trades." Andy shook his head and eyed Danielle suspiciously. "What are you now, an electrician?"

"I...know a little about electrical stuff," Danielle said. "Hazards of one of my past careers."

He turned his attention to Millie. "I've been looking for you. We need to head down to the karaoke stage. I want to do a little rearranging to make more room. Since our first night was such a huge success, I think we'll have a larger crowd tonight."

"When do I get to host karaoke?" Danielle whined.

Andy gave her a dark look. "I thought you were trying to get out of my department."

"True, but in the meantime, I still gotta do my job," Danielle said. "You've put me in charge of hosting the singles Mix & Mingle every week."

"That's because you're single," Andy pointed out.

"So is Millie," Danielle argued.

"Not really," Andy shook his head.

"Yes, I am," Millie countered. "I am single."

An uncomfortable silence filled the air.

"Well." Andy clasped his hands together. "It's settled. Let's head down to the stage." He grasped Millie under the elbow and steered her away from Annette and Danielle.

"I'm sorry Millie," Andy said when they were out of earshot. "I thought you and Captain Armati patched things up."

Millie stopped abruptly in the hall. "Patched things up? What's there to patch up? He's abandoning ship. Hasta la vista, baby."

"There's nothing he can do about it, Millie. He asked for the transfer to avoid a scandal on board the ship and now he has to transfer to Baroness of the Seas or risk losing his job."

"What scandal? So Luigi Falco filed a complaint." Millie began walking again. "It's just that he should've told me before I had to find out in front of a room full of strangers."

"I'm not a stranger."

"You know what I mean." They had reached deck five and the karaoke stage. Millie moved to a safer subject, one that didn't make her want to burst into tears. "So what's your plan?"

Andy and Millie stood in front of the stage. "I was thinking if we shifted the stage a little to the left, closer to the guest services desk, we could have maintenance bring in a few more lounge chairs and slide everything back, which would create a large dance floor area plus add more seating."

Millie held up a hand. "Shh. Did you hear that?"

"Hear what?"

"It's a buzzing noise," Millie said.

"I don't hear anything." Andy nudged a cluster of wires near his foot.

"I wouldn't touch those wires," Millie said. "Let me call Marcus in electrical." She unclipped her walkie-talkie from her belt, lifted it to her face and pressed the button. "Marcus T, do you copy?"

The radio crackled and finally Marcus answered. "This is Marcus."

"This is Millie Sanders. I'm on deck five in front of guest services with Andy Walker, the

Cruise Director. I need you to stop by ASAP please."

There was a brief silence. "10-4. I'm on my way."

Marcus, accompanied by Filip, the second electrician who had also worked on the karaoke stage and set up, arrived a short time later. "Whatcha got Miss Millie?"

"Maybe I'm being paranoid, but I hear a faint buzzing noise." She led the two men around the side of the newly constructed stage to the back and a cluster of wires. "It's coming from somewhere over here."

Millie pointed down, afraid to get too close. She remembered how the inside of the electrical panel had looked, and how Danielle had described what would happen if a person got too close and there was an electrical arc.

"I don't hear anything." Filip shook his head.

Andy hovered behind them. "I didn't hear anything either."

"I swear I heard it," Millie insisted. The sound of laughter and clink of glasses from the bar area echoed in the cavernous space. "It's too noisy in here."

Andy shook his head and frowned. "I'm sorry to bother you fellas. I'm sure you have more important things to do." He shot Millie a dark stare.

Marcus shook his head. "No sir. Since the...accident, we've had lots of calls from jittery crewmembers." He shrugged. "Better safe than sorry."

Marcus patted Millie's shoulder. "You call whenever you're concerned, Miss Millie." He shifted to the side and started to step over the wires when he stopped in his tracks.

"Wait! I think I heard something, too." Marcus took a step back, leaned forward and peered at a power strip, full of plug-ins. "It's coming from there." He glanced at Filip. "Kill the power in zone eight."

Filip nodded and hurried over to the far wall where he opened a panel box. Moments later, the atrium went dark.

"Whoa!" Small gasps and murmurs filled the atrium and grew louder as passengers became alarmed at the sudden lack of light.

"Great," Andy mumbled. "It's okay folks," he added in a loud voice. "The power will be back on in just a moment. Don't panic." He turned to Marcus. "Hurry up before the passengers freak out and stampede the place."

"Yes boss." Marcus bent down, grabbed the power strip and then jerked his hand back. "This strip is hot to the touch. I'm surprised it hasn't caught fire."

Chapter 17

"Quick, unplug it from the wall," Marcus instructed Filip, who traced the power supply to a large cluster of outlets on the other side of guest services.

"It's out," Filip said.

"Switch the power back on."

Filip hurried to the box, flipped the switch and bright lights, followed by the whir of equipment came to life.

Marcus picked up the power strip, holding it near the center as he studied the strip. "This could have been very bad."

"Bad as in set the place on fire bad?" Millie asked.

"Yes and also the risk of someone being electrocuted."

Marcus pointed to the plug-ins. "See these? This strip, the voltage is too high for this strip to handle."

"Why would someone use this power strip if it wasn't safe?" Andy asked. "I'm surprised the ship allows them to be used."

"They don't, Mr. Andy. All the ships power strips are required to have the automatic trip so that it shuts off if it gets too much juice." Marcus turned the strip so Andy and Millie could see the front. "This one is not ours. It doesn't have the button to automatically shut off the power supply."

"So you're saying you did not put this strip here?" Millie asked.

"No Miss Millie. I did not and I checked every wire the other day when you and I were here setting up." Millie could vouch for the fact. Marcus and she had done a thorough inspection.

"I will report this to Carmine right away." Marcus shifted the power strip to his other hand and bent down to inspect the plugs. "None of these plugs were damaged so I'll get someone down here to put in the right power strip and test it for safety."

Millie waited for Marcus and Filip to leave the area. "Why would someone intentionally switch out a safe power strip for an unsafe power strip?"

"It doesn't make sense. Maybe we have a fire bug or a serial killer on the loose," Andy said. "I'll need to report this to Captain Armati and Donovan Sweeney." The two finished discussing the changes to the karaoke area and all the while, in the back of her mind, Millie couldn't shake the feeling she was the killer's next target.

"Are you sure you're not too rattled for karaoke?" Andy asked. "I could switch you and Danielle."

"No," Millie shook her head. "It's okay. If it's my turn to go, it's my turn to go."

"I agree, but none of us needs a helping hand," Andy said. "I better head to the bridge to chat with Captain Armati."

Andy left Millie staring at the stage, trying to remember if she'd told the audience she would be back for another round that evening. She remembered how Felix, one of the dancers, had co-hosted the karaoke. Perhaps he would be able to remember.

Millie stepped inside the empty theater and made her way to the back. Felix could be in any number of places, assisting in guest activities. The dancers didn't carry radios, unless they were working on special assignments.

Most of the entertainment staff worked the lido deck for the dance parties and other guest participation contests, so Millie started there. She found Felix hosting a miniature golf contest on deck twelve and waited off to the side for the contest to wrap up.

After the contest ended and the participants departed, Millie stepped onto the putting green and made her way over to Felix, who smiled as she approached. "We still on for another night of Killer Karaoke this evening?"

"Aptly named," Millie groaned.

"Huh?"

"Nothing." Millie waved her hand. "I have a question. The other night when you helped host the karaoke, did I happen to mention whether or not I would be hosting it again this evening?"

"Hmm." Felix leaned on the golf club and stared out at the waves. "Yes. I think you did. Don't you remember telling the passengers that you wanted to make it a 70's disco / trivia / karaoke competition because it was one of your favorite eras?"

"You're right." Millie snapped her fingers. "I remember now. Thanks Felix. I'll see you later."

"I wouldn't miss it for the world." Felix winked at Millie. "I hear they're expecting an even larger crowd after word spread how much fun we had the other night."

A passenger approached to ask Felix a question about the salsa dance class, and Millie slipped away, certain now she was the intended target.

Patterson needed to hurry up and figure out who killed Luigi Falco. If not, there might be more victims and one of them Millie!

***

"There you are."

Millie pulled her keycard from the cabin door and waited while Danielle hurried toward her. "I tried radioing you but you didn't answer."

Millie glanced at her radio and noticed she had accidentally turned the volume all the way down, a big no-no when she was on duty. "Sorry. What's up?"

"I heard you and Andy were up checking out the karaoke set up with the electricians and all of the sudden the lights went out."

"There was a problem with one of the power strips," Millie explained as she pushed the cabin door open and stepped inside, holding it for Danielle.

"What kind of problem?" Danielle asked.

Millie told Danielle what Marcus had said.

"So you think someone was trying to zap you?" Danielle's eyes widened.

"Either that or we have an attempted serial killer on the loose." Millie dropped her lanyard on the small desk and slid onto the chair. "Is this day over yet?"

"Not by a longshot. So are you interested in hosting the singles' Mix and Mingles party while I host Killer Karaoke?" Danielle asked.

"No way." Millie shook her head. "I wouldn't want to chance my best bud getting electrocuted."

Danielle snorted. "Nice try." Her expression grew serious. "It seems to me that one of the electricians is behind all of this. It has to be someone who has a fair amount of knowledge about electrical stuff and is able to roam freely around the ship."

"They would definitely have to know the ship's layout," Millie said. She lifted a finger. "We've got Carmine, Marcus, Paloma and I'm adding Filip, one of the other electricians who helped work on the karaoke equipment."

"You could talk to Nikki Tan," Danielle suggested. "She has a bird's-eye view of the karaoke stage from behind guest services.

"Good idea." Millie glanced at her watch. "If someone intentionally tried to set the stage for another electrocution and they realized their plan backfired, what do you think the chances are they will try again?"

Danielle shrugged. "If you're sure it's not a coincidence, then I would imagine there will be another attempt." She brightened. "If somebody is out to do you in, we can set up a sting, catch them in the act."

"How?"

"I'm sure Annette has some surveillance equipment suited for this type of mission," Danielle said. "All you gotta do is set the trap. I'll take a run by the galley before heading to the singles hoopla to see what I can come up with."

She hurried on. "Later this evening, we sneak back to the area after the atrium bar closes for an old-fashioned stakeout."

It didn't sound like a foolproof plan to Millie, but they were short on time not to mention options. After tonight, the ship had one more night before docking in the home port of Miami.

If Patterson wasn't able to nail down a clear suspect, there was a good chance the authorities would remove Andy from the ship and charge him with Luigi Falco's murder.

***

Andy had been right, and Killer Karaoke was an even bigger success than before. Millie quickly decided Felix was the perfect co-host and she wasn't sure who had more fun, the guests or her and her partner.

Passengers packed the dance floor for the disco-era music and even managed to drag Millie and Felix onto the dancefloor to join in the festivities.

By the time karaoke ended, Millie's feet were sore and her voice hoarse. After the last passenger drifted off, the pair packed up the equipment and wandered off the stage.

"That was loads of fun," Felix said.

"It was, hands down, my favorite hosting event ever." Millie gave Felix a quick hug and told him she couldn't wait for next time, before limping back to her cabin to get ready for the stakeout.

Chapter 18

Annette slipped the small camera behind the brochure display on top of the excursion desk and then pulled her cell phone from her pocket before turning it on. "Needs to go a little to the left." She reached up and shifted the device. "Perfect."

"Aren't you afraid someone is going to see this, steal it or worse yet, turn it in?" Millie whispered as she crouched behind the desk.

"Not at all." Annette shook her head. "The excursion desk won't be open until we dock in Miami since there aren't any more port stops." She studied her phone. "I could use one more device on the other side, by guest services, but there's no way the second one will go undetected unless we attach it to something." She lifted her head and stared at the desk on the other side of the room. "It's too risky. This will have to do."

"Now what?" Danielle asked.

"We wait," Annette said. "You might as well make yourself comfy." She shifted to a sitting position, scooched back and leaned against the wall.

Millie gazed at her watch. It was midnight. They had decided to stake out the karaoke area for a couple hours, or until they were too tired to stay awake. Without a set of eyes watching the stage, they wouldn't catch anything. Annette would have to record any suspicious activity on her phone.

"I'm hungry," Danielle muttered. "I wish I had brought a snack."

"I've been experimenting on a fabulous new sandwich for the deli I plan to roll out soon. You can come up and taste test in the morning if you want," Annette offered.

"You mean we can be your guinea pigs?" Millie teased. "I'll try it."

"Me too," Danielle said.

The trio grew quiet and the faint strains of music from the late night dance club, Tahitian Nights, drifted down.

"I'm bored." Danielle yawned.

"You don't have to stay," Millie said. "Not all sleuthing involves rappelling down the sides of cruise ships or leading suspects into the Mayan jungle."

"Or swinging over the sides of balconies and crawling through ventilation systems," Danielle shot back.

"Touché."

"Shush. I hear someone coming." Annette held a finger to her lips.

Millie sucked in a breath and turned her ear. There was someone coming. She could hear the sharp click of their heels on the tile floors. The sound was coming from the hall, leading into the atrium area.

"We're running out of time, captain." The voice belonged to Purser Donovan Sweeney, whose office was located directly behind guest services.

"Patterson isn't making any progress?" Captain Armati asked.

"I talked to him earlier this evening, sir. He said he's following up on several leads but admitted he might not finish his investigation before we dock in Miami." Donovan's voice faded and then a door shut.

Danielle placed her forehead in the palm of her hand. "We're running out of time. If we...or they, can't figure out who killed Falco, Andy is on the hook." She turned to Millie. "They'll probably put you in charge as acting cruise director and me as assistant cruise director."

The statement sent a bolt of fear down Millie's spine. She was not prepared to take over as cruise director. Andy's shoes were too big to fill. Not only that, Danielle was in no way, shape or form ready to take on the role of assistant cruise director. They needed to figure out who had murdered Falco and tried to electrocute Millie earlier that evening and they needed to move fast.

"I'll march down to Patterson's office first thing tomorrow morning," Millie said. "Right after I stop by the galley to taste Annette's newest creation."

The trio stayed hidden behind the excursions desk for another hour, waiting for Donovan and the captain to leave Donovan's office. Finally, Millie began to nod off and they called it a night.

Danielle offered to camp out for a while longer, just in case someone showed up but the other two agreed it was more than likely a waste of time.

"Are you going to take the camera?" Millie asked Annette.

"Nah. I got about a dozen of them. Bought 'em in bulk when they were buy one, get one free." Annette waved a hand. "I'll come back for it tomorrow."

When they reached the crew quarters, Annette turned right at the bottom of the stairs while Millie and Danielle made a left. It had been another failed mission and Millie was growing frustrated. Captain Armati had one foot out the door, or in his case, down the gangway and Andy's career, not to mention his freedom, was in jeopardy.

She wondered why he didn't seem more concerned. Maybe he had faith Patterson would come through. Millie couldn't sit back and watch as her friend, her mentor, was arrested and removed from the ship. She knew Andy hadn't killed Luigi and maybe that's why Andy was taking it so calmly. He knew he was innocent and believed somehow justice would prevail.

After she climbed into bed and tucked the covers under her chin, she squeezed her eyes shut and prayed for a break in the case. She prayed for Andy, for Cat, who was making progress on her road to recovery and, last, but not least, she prayed God would heal her broken heart.

It took some time before Millie was able to drift off to sleep and after she did, she dreamt she was back in the jungle, chasing after Danielle, who was, once again, in imminent danger.

She had several other jumbled dreams and finally woke with a lingering feeling something was about to happen.

Millie climbed out of bed and tiptoed to the bathroom.

Danielle was awake by the time Millie emerged. "What a restless night." Danielle lifted her hands above her head and attempted to stretch, but the low ceiling was in the way so she hopped off her bunk and tried again. "What's your schedule for this morning?"

"The first thing I'm going to do is head to the galley to see what new recipe Annette has concocted. After that, I'm going to run by Dave Patterson's office before I start my shift."

Millie made her way over to the small desk, picked up her schedule for the day and then grabbed her reading glasses before slipping them on. "Group cycling up on the sports deck?" she moaned. "Now I think Andy is trying to kill *me*."

"Nah," Danielle smiled. "It's fun. I did it the other day. You'll survive. It's a stationary bike."

"I've got the behind the scenes tour," Danielle said.

Millie wrinkled her nose. "Andy is letting you host the tour?"

"No. I'm there to watch and observe, which means I'll be with Andy during the tour so you're free to do a little more sleuthing."

"Good point." Millie waited for Danielle to use the bathroom first. She turned the television on and watched as Andy broadcast his morning show, ticking off the list of events on board the ship for their last fun-filled day at sea. He looked so calm, cool and collected.

Danielle popped out of the bathroom. "It's all yours."

Millie stood. "Say. That picture you took when we were inside Paloma's cabin, the one of her and Marcus. Can I take a look at it again?"

"Sure." Danielle opened her closet door, dropped her dirty clothes inside and then headed to her bunk where she stuck her hand under her pillow and pulled out her cell phone. She pressed the screen, fiddled with the front and then handed it to Millie.

Millie turned the phone so she had a clearer view and studied the photo. It was blurry and she tapped the screen to enlarge the picture. She'd only met Paloma the one time and something about her, something Millie couldn't quite put her finger on, looked different.

The couple was standing close to the railing on one of the upper decks. The Castillo San Cristóbal, also known as Fort San Cristóbal, located in Old San Juan Puerto Rico was behind them. She could tell the picture wasn't very old and had been taken on board the ship.

Siren of the Seas had recently switched itineraries from the Bahamas, South Seas Cay, the cruise line's private island, and Grand Cayman, to the current itinerary, which included San Juan, St. Thomas and St. Croix.

"Can you send a copy of this to my phone?" Millie asked.

"Sure." Danielle took the cell phone from Millie. "But not until we get into port. I need cell service to connect."

"True. Make sure you don't delete the photo," Millie said as she headed to the bathroom.

When she emerged a short time later, Danielle was pacing the floor. "We need to hurry up if we plan to stop by Annette's place before starting our shifts."

Millie grimaced. "I have a feeling this is going to be a very long day."

Chapter 19

Danielle and Millie strode out of the cabin and headed up the stairs to the galley. Although it was still early, Millie knew Annette was already in her kitchen. In fact, Millie suspected there were days when Annette spent every waking hour in the galley and would be perfectly content to bunk there.

Millie heard Annette before she saw her. Amit was standing across from her and they were hovering over a large platter.

The smell of freshly baked bread wafted in the air and Millie sniffed appreciatively.

"The taste testers have arrived," Danielle said breezily as she made her way around the maze of counters while Millie followed behind.

Amit and Annette had amassed a small assembly line of food, which included slices of sourdough bread, shaved turkey and thick slices of bacon. "What are you making?" Millie asked as she patted her stomach and eyed the food.

"Creamy pesto turkey bacon Paninis," Amit replied as he slathered a thick layer of butter on a slice of freshly baked bread.

Annette reached for a chopping block and knife. "We're sending samples to the deli crew this morning but you get to try it first," she said as she chopped two cloves of garlic.

Annette dropped the cloves inside a nearby blender and then added parmesan cheese, olive oil, basil, lemon juice and whipped cream cheese.

"Now for the last ingredient," she said as she dumped a small bowl of chopped nuts on top of the mixture. Annette flipped the switch and the machine began to whir.

When the ingredients had reached the consistency of a soft, creamy paste, she removed the cover. "I forgot the salt and pepper." She added some salt and pepper and blended it one last time.

Annette removed the cover, grabbed a butter knife and scooped a heaping mound out before spreading an even layer on the other side of the bread Amit had buttered.

Amit carefully placed the bread, butter side down, on the top of the Panini press, added slices of turkey and bacon, and then started to add pieces of artichoke hearts.

Danielle held up a hand. "I'll pass on the artichoke hearts. They give me gas."

"TMI," Millie groaned.

Amit grinned. "Yes ma'am." He added them to the three other sandwiches, and then covered them with another slice of bread, butter side up.

Annette lowered the lid on the press and held it down.

The bread sizzled and melted cheese oozed down the sides. "The breakfast of champions," Millie joked.

When the sandwiches were grilled to perfection, Annette lifted the lid while Amit slipped a spatula under the sandwiches, placing each sandwich on a small dinner plate.

After Annette cut the sandwiches in half, she slid a plate toward the other three and eased the last one in front of her.

"This looks delish," Danielle gushed. She reached for the hot-off-the-press sandwich while Millie folded her hands and bowed her head.

"Whoops! I forgot." Danielle dropped her sandwich and followed suit, folding her hands and bowing her head.

Millie sucked in a breath. "Dear Lord. Thank you for this food. Thank you for all of your gifts, our health, our jobs, our friendships. I pray Lord, that we live our lives as an example of You and that Your light shines in us. Amen."

"Amen," the others echoed in unison.

Millie took a big bite of her sandwich and chewed with gusto. The combination of garlic and basil, and the creaminess of the cream cheese, along with the smoked meat melted in her mouth. She gobbled her first half before taking a breather and reaching for a nearby coffee carafe and clean mug.

She poured a cup of piping hot coffee and took a sip as she eyed her half-eaten sandwich. "This sandwich is delicious," she said. "If the deli guys don't like this, they need to have their heads examined."

As they ate, they discussed the case and the previous evening's unsuccessful attempt to uncover the killer.

Danielle tore a chunk of sandwich off and popped it in her mouth. "What if it isn't one of the electricians? I mean, I'm not an electrician and I still know enough about it to be dangerous."

Millie snapped her fingers. "And the killer is trying to frame the electrical crew to lead the investigators in the wrong direction."

"The internet is a powerful tool," Annette added. "Think about all the information you can find online without ever having to take a class or hire someone." She reached for her napkin and dabbed the corner of her mouth. "I doubt a passenger is responsible for Luigi Falco's death. I'd bet my life it's a staff or crewmember, and if they're not a professional electrician, they would have had to do a little research to do the deed."

"Which means they would have had to use the crew computers to research," Millie finished. "I wish I knew how to hack into passwords so we could take a look at what's been researched online."

Annette dropped her dirty napkin on top of her empty plate. "I just so happen to have a little hacking background from my former life." She gripped the edge of her plate and spun it in a circle. "It's been a few years, but I reckon I could maneuver my way through a few internet back doors."

Amit carried his empty plate to the dishwasher and placed it inside. "I better get back to work before the boss fires me." He winked at Annette and wandered to the other side of the kitchen, to the salad prep area.

Millie was the second to finish her sandwich. "I guess I was hungrier than I thought." She carried her empty plate to the sink, rinsed it off and then stuck it inside the dishwasher. "Annette, someday you're going to fess up and tell us who you are."

Annette wandered over to the sink. She patted Millie on the shoulder before she turned the galley faucet on and rinsed the crumbs from her plate. "I'd love to tell you, my friend..."

Millie finished her sentence. "I know, but then you'd have to kill me." She glanced at the clock on the galley wall. "There's just enough time for me to have a quick chat with Dave Patterson before I have to check in with Andy." She shifted her gaze. "So what time do you want to meet in the employee lounge to hack into the computers?"

The trio discussed their schedules, agreeing they all had breaks around three o'clock. The only concern was other crewmembers or staff might be in the employee lounge and on the computers while they were trying to spy.

It was a hurdle they'd have to face when they got there.

Annette returned to the counter to finish assembling the remainder of the Paninis earmarked for the deli crew's taste test while Millie and Danielle stepped out of the galley and into the hall. "Where you headed?" Millie asked the younger woman.

"Behind the scenes tour with Andy, remember?" Danielle replied. "Then I'm scheduled to work at the Teen Scene for the rest of the morning. The teens are trying to teach me to 'Flip the Funk.'"

Millie frowned. "Flip the Funk? What in the world?"

"You know." Danielle began waving her arms and tapping her feet. *"Git down low and swing your arms. Git down and flip the funk ...flip the funk."*

"Those kids sure come up with some crazy dances." Millie rolled her eyes. "Remind me to never volunteer for the Teen Scene. I'd try that move and end up in traction," she joked.

Danielle grinned and then her gaze shifted as she stared over Millie's shoulder. The color drained from her face. "Casey?"

Casey...Millie recognized the name. It was the name Danielle uttered in the middle of the night when she was having a bad dream. It had happened again the previous week, and despite Millie's attempts to get Danielle to talk about 'Casey,' she always shut down, refusing to discuss either her nightmares or whoever 'Casey' was.

Millie spun around and stared down the corridor. Standing in front of the gift shop was a young man, in his late 20's if she had to guess. His hair was light, an almost platinum blond color.

The passenger must've felt their eyes on him because he turned and stared at them, at Danielle. She took a step forward. "I..." She slowly walked forward. When she got close, she stopped in her tracks and her shoulders slumped.

Millie trailed behind. The women stood side by side as the young man and the group he was with wandered in the opposite direction and disappeared from sight. "Danielle, who is Casey?" she asked in a soft, low voice.

Danielle turned, her blue eyes brimming with unshed tears. "It's." Her lower lip trembled. "Casey *was* my younger brother. He died a couple years ago." Unchecked tears trailed down Danielle's cheeks and Millie led her off to the side, out of the stream of foot traffic.

Danielle swiped at her tears. "It's my fault he's dead," she whispered. "I couldn't save him."

Millie closed her eyes and for a brief moment, she could almost feel the young woman's pain. She quickly opened them. "I'm sorry Danielle." She didn't know what else to say and although she wanted to talk to Danielle, this wasn't the place. They both had to head to their activities.

Instead, Millie squeezed Danielle's hand. "We're going to talk about this later, when we're alone, but I know you, Danielle. You're as loyal as they come. You're a caring, wonderful young woman and I am certain you didn't kill your brother."

It was getting late. If Millie didn't hurry, she'd be late for work, having already missed her opportunity to chat with Patterson, which would have to wait until after her group cycling class.

Danielle's lower lip trembled and she nodded. "I need to meet Andy for the behind the scenes tour." She dabbed at her eyes with the back of her shirtsleeve. "Is my face all red?"

"Yes and so is your nose. You look like a total wreck," Millie smiled. "I'm teasing. You look beautiful as usual." She reached over and gave Danielle a quick hug. "Get going before Andy sends a search party to look for you."

Danielle nodded and hurried toward the library, where the tour group was scheduled to meet while Millie headed to the gym for her cycling class.

By the time Millie finished the class, she was sweating profusely; convinced Andy was trying to take her out.

Even though the workout required another shower, Millie still had enough free time before her next activity, the arts and crafts class, to swing by Dave Patterson's office.

When Millie reached the security office, the door was closed, but she could see through the frosted glass pane the lights were on. She lightly tapped on the glass and heard a muffled response so she eased the door open and stuck her head around the corner.

Dave Patterson was inside, talking on the walkie-talkie. He motioned Millie inside and she slid into the seat closest to the door while she waited for him to finish his conversation.

"10-4. I'll look into it. I'm sure our assistant cruise director has a very plausible reason as to why she was spotted entering one of the housekeeping staff's cabins."

Chapter 20

Millie's heart began to thump in her chest. She'd been certain no one had spotted Danielle and her sneaking into Paloma and Hazelle's cabin!

Patterson turned the volume down on the walkie-talkie and slowly set it on the edge of his desk before he folded his hands and leaned back in his chair. "You must have read my mind."

He pointed to the walkie-talkie. "That was Kimel Pang, head of our housekeeping department. He said one of the housekeeping staff spotted you and another woman entering Paloma Herdez's cabin. He described the other woman as a young staff member with long blonde hair, pulled back in a ponytail."

Patterson clasped his hands and tapped his index fingers together as he studied Millie.

She squirmed in her chair and the tips of her ears burned. Millie's mind searched for some sort of plausible explanation, but she knew there was none.

He went on. "There aren't too many young, blonde female employees on board this ship, other than a couple of the dancers and your sidekick, Danielle Kneldon."

"I." Millie decided there was no sense in trying to defend her actions. "Yes. Danielle and I entered Paloma's cabin. We searched her cabin for clues after finding out Luigi Falco and Paloma had been seeing each other."

Patterson sighed heavily as he shook his head. "I'm going to have to write you up. You cannot prowl around this ship, using your special privileges to snoop on people. I'll have to report this to Andy and Donovan Sweeney, too."

"Okay," she said in a small voice. "I was just trying to..."

"Save Andy's hide." Patterson held up a hand. "I know, Millie, and I admire you for your loyalty to Andy, but rules are made for a reason."

Patterson droned on about protocol, acceptable behavior, overstepping one's position. Millie's mind began to wander as she wondered if Falco's death would not only be the end of Andy's career, but hers as well.

"Are you close to figuring out who murdered Luigi Falco?" Millie interrupted. She remembered the conversation between Donovan Sweeney and the captain the previous night.

"We have some leads we're following up on."

"But you're running out of time. If you don't have a clear suspect by the time this ship docks tomorrow, Andy is history." Millie made a slicing motion across her neck.

"Luigi had his share of enemies including his own boss," Patterson admitted. "We've questioned Carmine at length but he appears to have an airtight alibi and had not even been near the theater. His co-workers, Marcus and Filip did, as well."

Patterson leaned forward. "Did you find anything inside Paloma's cabin?"

"Yep." Millie nodded.

"And?"

"I just got lectured for searching the woman's cabin, which, by the way, ought to be condemned by the sanitation crew, and now you want me to tell you what I found?" Millie decided to play hardball. "What's in it for me?"

Patterson leaned back, a slow smile creeping across his face. "Beneath that sweet, Midwestern exterior is a tough-as-nails lady. Okay, I'll bite. What *is* in it for you?"

The ball was in Millie's court and she wasn't about to blow it. "I want to keep my special access card. I don't mind a written reprimand as long as it is expunged after..." Her voice trailed off. How long did she want to remain on probation? "Three months," she finished.

"Three months if you have something good. Six months if you tell me something I already know," Patterson bargained.

"It's a deal. Same for Danielle," Millie bargained.

"Okay. What did you find?"

"Other than a disgusting, smelly cabin, we found a note tucked behind the mirror. It was addressed to a Maria Falco in Cochem, Germany."

Patterson raised a brow so Millie knew it was information he didn't already have.

She continued. "There was a cell phone inside the desk and on the phone was a blurry picture of what looked like Paloma. She was cozying up to Marcus. The picture was recent. It was taken on board the Siren of the Seas and the backdrop was the fort in Old San Juan."

"Three months probation." Patterson reached inside his left hand desk drawer, pulled out a clipboard, attached a form and grabbed an ink pen. "I'm going to write you up for unapproved access to crew quarters and if you keep your nose clean for the next three months, the document will be shredded."

Millie sat quietly while he continued to write. When he finished, he slid the clipboard, along with the pen, across the desk. "Sign on the bottom."

Millie signed above the spot where Patterson had printed her name, dated it and slid it back. "That seems fair. I think I can behave myself for three months." She stood. "Oh, by the way, Danielle took a picture of the picture. It's on her phone."

"She's next on my list," Patterson said. "I'll track her down later."

"I guess you've ruled out an accidental death." Millie shuffled to the side as she headed to the door before turning back. "I suppose you don't want to share with me who you think killed Luigi Falco."

"You know I can't divulge that information, Millie. I would tell you to stay out of this, but I know it's too late." Patterson stood. "How 'bout this? Don't drag anyone else into your investigation."

Millie held up three fingers. "I promise. Scout's honor. I won't involve anyone else who hasn't already gotten involved." She didn't wait for a reply as she opened the door, stepped out into the hall and quietly closed it behind her.

***

The rest of the afternoon flew by as Millie flitted from arts and crafts to trivia to bingo to salsa lessons and then finally took a late lunch, right before she planned to meet up with Annette and Danielle for their search of the crew's internet computers.

The ship's food theme for the day was Indian, which wasn't Millie's favorite. She made her way to the back of the buffet line and grabbed a dinner plate and a tray.

The first item to catch her attention was *malai kofta*. Her eyes squinted as she read the description, *fried cheese balls in creamy gravy*. Millie liked fried cheese and she liked gravy so decided to try it as she scooped two balls onto the edge of her plate.

Next in line was *aloo Shimla mirch*. The placard described it as cooked potatoes with green bell pepper, both of which Millie liked so she added that to her plate.

She wrinkled her nose at the next offering, *gosht palak,* a spinach and sheep mutton curry.

Deciding two new dishes were adventurous enough, Millie made a beeline for the deli in the back where she ordered a sloppy joe on a soft roll, complete with a pickle spear and side of fresh coleslaw.

The dining room was virtually empty and she made her way to her favorite table in the far corner. She unfolded her napkin and placed it in her lap before bowing her head to pray, thanking God she hadn't gotten into too much trouble for sneaking into Paloma's cabin.

When she lifted her head, Captain Armati was standing on the other side of the table, silently watching her.

"Hello Millie. Do you have a minute?" He didn't wait for a reply as he pulled out the chair across from her and sat. "Don't let me interrupt. You eat and I'll talk."

Millie nodded and reached for her pickle spear.

"I've sent a second request to Majestic Cruise Line's headquarters, asking for permission to remain on board Siren of the Seas."

Millie stopped chewing and stared. "You did?"

"Yes." He nodded.

"I don't know what to say," Millie said.

"Say you'll join me for dinner this evening in my apartment."

"I..."

"I'll take that as a yes," the captain said. "What is your schedule for the rest of the day?"

Millie thought of the plan to search the internet later with Annette and Danielle. "I'm not sure." She reached inside her pocket, pulled out her daily schedule and then unfolded it. "I'm off during the dinner hour, six to seven and then I have to head back to help out with the "Fond Farewell" party, which starts at 7:30.

"Good." The captain nodded.

"Captain Armati, do you copy?" The captain's radio began squawking.

"Never a moment's peace," Captain Armati said as he reached for his radio. "Go ahead Antonio."

"We need you in the bridge."

"Be right there." He clipped his radio to his belt and stood. "See you at six?"

"O-of course," Millie said.

The captain nodded and turned on his heel as he headed out of the buffet area.

Millie hurriedly finished her lunch. She took one bite of the fried cheese balls and decided the sauce was not to her liking. The potatoes with green bell pepper were tasty and she ate the entire dish.

After she finished her food, she carried her empty dishes to the exit where she placed the plate inside the bin and dropped the napkin beside it.

Danielle and Annette were already waiting for her outside the employee computer/lounge area when she got there. She glanced through the glass window and was relieved there was no one inside.

"Let's get this show on the road." Millie opened the outer door and held it while Annette and Danielle stepped inside.

Annette surveyed the six computer stations and made her way over to the one on the far side. She settled into a chair that faced the entrance. "We can keep an eye on whoever comes in."

"Good idea." Danielle eased into the chair on Annette's left and Millie took the one on the right.

Annette tapped the keyboard and then swiped her card to access her account. A box popped up, asking for Annette's password. She leaned forward, blocking Millie's view but not Danielle's view.

"Oh. My. Gosh," Danielle gasped. "Tell me you didn't type 'Rag Team NSA.'"

Annette's fingers froze. She gazed at Danielle out of the corner of her eye. "Is there something you haven't told me?" Annette's eyes bore into Danielle's eyes.

Danielle stared back. "NSA," Danielle and Annette said in unison.

Millie was confused. "What is NSA?"

Annette lowered her voice, peering over the top of the computer to make sure they were still alone. "National Security Agency, or in this case..."

Danielle finished her sentence. "Agent."

"National Security Agent?" Millie blinked rapidly. "As in U.S. Government agent?"

She leaned forward in her chair. "Are you a government agent?" Millie asked Annette before shifting her gaze to Danielle. "And you too?"

Millie's head started to spin as she stared at two people she no longer knew. Small pieces began to fall into place. The jokes the captain had made about Annette. There was the fact

Annette was a sharp shooter, a female ninja, a weapons expert, not to mention a computer hack.

Then there was Danielle, who was an expert weapons handler, who knew a lot about electrical, as well as investigations. Millie rested her forehead in the palm of her hand.

"We'll discuss this later." Annette turned her attention to the computer screen and began typing again. It all looked Greek to Millie as her friend entered unique number and letter combinations.

Every once in a while, Danielle would add her two cents and Millie could only guess Danielle also had some computer-hacking knowledge.

"There it is," Annette announced as she jabbed her index finger on the screen of the computer. "The needle in the haystack. Someone used one of these computers to research death by electrocution."

Millie slipped her reading glasses on and peered at the screen. She was right. There on the screen was an entire in-depth article about wiring and electrocution. "Can you tell when someone researched it?" Millie asked.

"Yes. It appears to have been a week ago yesterday at 2:53 in the morning," Annette said. "This means the person snuck down here when they were certain everyone else was in bed so they wouldn't be spotted."

"Wouldn't be spotted using the computer," Danielle added. "In case someone...a hacker or computer geek took a look at the files."

"So it looks as if the killer may not have had a background in electrical engineering," Millie mused.

"Or it's a red herring to throw the authorities off, who may have already covered this angle and checked the crew's computer access," Annette pointed out.

"True." Millie shook her head. "So we're back to square one."

The women discussed the photo of Paloma and Marcus, the letter Danielle and Millie had found in Paloma's room as well as Carmine's reported obsession with Paloma.

"I'm going to ask Marcus point-blank if he had a thing for Paloma," Millie announced. "If I catch him off guard, he might slip up and say something."

Annette logged off the computer and started to stand, but Millie reached out and stopped her. "No one goes anywhere until you two spill the truth. Do you both work for the government?"

"No," Annette shook her head. "Not anymore." She told Millie and Danielle how she'd grown up in a military family, moving from town-to-town, country-to-country, while her father worked his way up the ranks.

The travel and being a military brat was in her blood and she joined the U.S. Armed Forces right out of high school where she discovered she had a knack for spying.

Annette's father and family friends pulled a few strings and she began her career working for the National Security Agency, traveling all over the world, wherever the agency sent her.

"Several years ago, I was involved in a particularly brutal takedown and, although I wasn't engaged in the gunfire, a child was killed in the crossfire." Annette stared at her clenched fists. "I held that dying child in my arms as the mother, who watched her child die, picked up a gun...the gun I had dropped when I tried to shield her child from the bullets and committed suicide."

Annette closed her eyes. "I still see that poor baby and still hear the mother's anguished screams." She opened her eyes. "After that, I lost my edge. I couldn't do it anymore."

"So you joined Siren of the Seas as the director of food and beverage?" Millie asked.

"I immersed myself in a prestigious culinary institute and discovered my second passion...food. After I finished, my former boss put in a good word for me and Captain Armati agreed to give me a chance."

She continued. "Plus, I'm a darn good cook, with the help of my trusty sidekick Amit," Annette said. She placed the palms of her hands on the desk and pushed herself up. "So that's my story. The captain knows, Donovan knows. I'm officially retired but as you know, they're still tempted at times to drag me into the fray."

"I don't help, either," Millie said.

Annette patted her shoulder. "I believe God sent you here for a reason and one of those reasons was to let me know it ain't over yet. There's still a little adventure and purpose left for Annette Delacroix." She turned to Danielle. "What's your story young lady?"

Danielle shrugged. "I grew up in a military family and heard the term more than a few times, that's all," she answered vaguely.

"I see you're not ready to talk." Annette slid the chair under the desk. "We all have skeletons in our closets and a life filled with regrets...that fraction of a second where you wish more than anything you could go back and change things, but we can't. We have to move forward."

The trio wandered out of the employee lounge and down the hall. They stopped in front of Danielle and Millie's cabin.

"Carpe diem. Seize the day," Annette said. "I better get upstairs before Amit launches a search party."

Danielle headed back to the cabin while Millie watched Annette march down the long corridor and disappear from sight. She decided, then and there, even if Captain Armati transferred to Baroness of the Seas, she was going to make the most of the time they had left.

Carpe diem.

Chapter 21

At 5:59 on the dot, Millie slipped inside the bridge. Staff Captain Vitale turned when he saw Millie cross the room. "It's good to see you Millie," he said.

"It's good to see you, too, Captain Vitale," she simply said before she made her way down the small hall that connected the bridge and the captain's apartment.

Millie tapped on the outer door and a couple seconds later, the door opened. A brown bundle of fur darted through the opening and pounced on her heeled shoe.

She picked Scout up and held him close, closing her eyes while he licked her face, her chin, the side of her neck and anywhere else his small, pink tongue could reach.

Finally, she set the wiggling pup down and he raced back inside. Captain Armati held the door and waited for Millie to step across the threshold. "He has missed you. I have missed you."

Before Millie could reply, the door closed. The captain pulled her into his arms and kissed her, slowly at first, but the kiss soon intensified until every fiber of Millie's body was on fire.

She began to feel lightheaded and placed both hands on his chest. Nic took this as an invitation and the kiss deepened.

When he finally pulled away, Millie was breathless. She pressed a hand to her throat and said the first thing that popped into her head. "I hope you don't greet every woman who comes into your apartment with a kiss."

Captain Armati...Nic...smiled. His dark smoldering eyes were mesmerizing. "No, just one beautiful, amazing woman who has been avoiding me." He stepped into the kitchen and returned a second later, a bouquet of long-stemmed red roses in his hand. "For you," he said.

"Oh my gosh. They're beautiful." Millie took the bouquet. She touched the tip of a rose with her finger and breathed in the fragrant aroma.

"We should put them in water until you take them home." He waved her into the kitchen where he filled a plastic drink cup with water and Millie placed the gorgeous bouquet inside.

Scout, who had followed them into the kitchen, began pawing at the back of Millie's ankle. She patted Scout's head and gave his ear a gentle tug. "Thank you, too."

"Come. Dinner is ready. I had the meal delivered early so we wouldn't be disturbed."

Millie followed Nic into the cozy dining room. A pale blue tablecloth covered the small, round table. In the center of the table a candelabrum with three tall, tapered candles gave the small room an intimate glow.

He pulled out Millie's chair and waited for her to sit before taking the seat across from her. "Our time is short, unfortunately, but next time I will order a special dinner we can savor out on the balcony," he promised.

Millie reached for her glass of water. "Will there be a next time?" His face fell and Millie wished she could take back the comment, but it was too late.

"God is in control. I've been praying about it," she confessed as she lifted her glass. "Here's to many more voyages across the ocean together."

The captain smiled and lifted his glass. "To many more."

Millie sipped her water and carefully set the glass next to her plate. "What are we having for dinner?"

"I chose a mixed salad and strawberry bisque soup. I remembered how you told me you loved strawberries," Nic said. "For our entrée, we have pan-seared halibut with lemon dill sauce."

"It sounds delicious." Millie said as she removed the covers from her soup and salad dishes.

The conversation was light and they stayed on safe topics, careful to avoid mentioning the elephant in the room...Nic's upcoming transfer.

They discussed the ports, the food and the entertainment schedule and even touched on Luigi Falco's demise. It seemed somewhat surreal to Millie that she was sitting across from a man she cared so much about, who was days away from leaving.

She forced the thoughts from her head and focused on the conversation.

Scout stopped by to beg for treats and Millie shared some chunks of her soft bread roll and a piece of fish.

Dessert was a tempting array of bite-size treats. She plucked a small cheesecake, topped with chocolate shavings from the tray and then poured coffee into two cups from a carafe sitting on the edge of the table.

Captain Armati decided on a miniature chocolate cupcake. He removed the wrapper and bit into it. "Very good," he mumbled between bites.

After they finished their desserts and a cup of coffee, he abruptly shoved back his chair and stood. "Come with me." He beckoned her out of her chair.

"Where?"

"The balcony."

Scout led the way as Nic and Millie trailed behind. The sun was setting and cast a soft, orange glow across the water. It was a beautiful Caribbean evening and the gentle ocean breeze made the salty sea air the perfect temperature.

Millie tilted her head and peered up at the suite balconies as she remembered Gloria and Liz's recent cruise. It seemed so long ago.

The captain moved closer and Millie turned to face him. She wondered if he was going to kiss her again and her pulse began to race.

"No matter what happens, Millie, I will be back. Don't give up on me so easily." He gazed into her eyes, his expression unreadable.

"I'm sorry I was avoiding you. It's just that I was shocked," she admitted.

"I wanted to tell you the other day when you stopped by, but I couldn't," he said. "By the time Andy said something, it was too late. I'm sorry, too."

He leaned forward, his lips gently brushing Millie's lips.

Millie wrapped her arms around his neck and drew him even closer. Time stood still as they remained locked in a loving embrace. Finally,

Millie leaned back and pressed the palms of her hands to her flushed cheeks. "I...I'm sorry."

Captain Armati grinned. "Sorry for what? I'm not sorry," he teased as he reached into his front pocket and pulled out a small jewelry box. "This is for you...my Millie."

Millie stared at the jewelry box.

"Don't you want to open it?" he asked.

"I-yes. Of course." Millie took the box from Nic and slowly lifted the lid.

Inside the box was a heart-shaped diamond necklace. Millie's fingers trembled as she carefully tugged on the silver chain, removing the dainty piece of jewelry from the box. "It's beautiful."

"It's a promise," Nic said. "Here, let me help." He took the necklace from Millie, unhooked the clasp and then reached around her before fastening it near the back of her neck. "It's my promise for our future, Millie."

Millie gazed at the heart. She flipped it over and rubbed her thumb over the back. She didn't have her reading glasses but could tell there was something etched on it. "I can't read the letters."

"Those are my initials. NDA. Niccolo Davide Armati." Nic tucked his hand under Millie's chin and lifted it so that their eyes met. "I love you," he whispered huskily. "I cannot ask you the question I want to but one day, hopefully soon, we can put this behind us and begin our life together."

Millie's eyes widened. "I..."

Captain Armati...Nic...leaned forward and gently kissed Millie. The kiss was a promise, his promise things would work out and they would have a future together.

A loud pounding on the outer door interrupted their moment and Nic reluctantly pulled back. "It is time to return to the real world."

Millie swallowed hard and absentmindedly touched the diamond studded heart necklace. "I love you too and I'm going to pray God works this out for us," she whispered softly.

Nic nodded before he grasped her hand and led her back inside. She stood near the dining room table as the captain hurried to the door and flung it open.

Captain Vitale stood on the other side. "I'm sorry to interrupt, but we have a crew member on deck, threatening to jump overboard."

Chapter 22

"Let's go." Captain Armati strode down the hall and into the bridge.

Millie hurried after Captain Vitale and Captain Armati, who picked up the pace and began jogging toward the exit door. "Where are they?"

"She's up on the bow of the ship, right next to the crew hot tub area," Vitale said breathlessly. "Patterson and Doctor Gundervan are up there now, trying to talk her into coming down."

Millie was certain she knew exactly who was up on the bow, threatening to jump. It was Paloma Herdez.

They hustled down the stairs, along a small hall, through a secret passageway marked "crew only" and emerged onto the bow of the ship.

The crew-only outdoor deck area was large. It included two hot tubs, a covered bar area and several lounge chairs. Millie had stopped by a few months back to check it out, but it wasn't her favorite crew-only area of the ship. She preferred spending her limited free time sleeping or reading...or with Captain Armati.

Her heart sank when she spotted the young woman, Paloma, teetering on the edge of the railing, gripping it with both hands. Her eyes were wild, and locked on Dave Patterson, who spoke to her in a low, soothing voice.

"You don't want to do this, Paloma," Patterson said softly. "You have so much to live for. Think of your family, think of your friends. If you come down, we'll help you. You're not alone."

A cluster of the ship's crew stood off to one side. Millie shifted her gaze, shaded her eyes and studied the upper decks. Several passengers had noticed, too, and began to gather along the railings.

"I did not kill Luigi," Paloma cried. "I loved him and he loved me."

"No one said you killed Luigi," Patterson said.

"It was Marcus. First, he after me, then he kill my boyfriend," she insisted. "He jealous of my b-."

Millie was certain she was about to say "baby" but caught herself before the words came out.

Doctor Gundervan, who was standing next to Patterson, reached out his hand. "Come down from there, Paloma."

Paloma stared at Gundervan's hand. She shifted her body and in that moment, she lost her grip and began to teeter back and forth.

Patterson lunged forward and grasped Paloma's upper arm, jerking her toward him and the safety of the ship. They both fell onto the deck. Patterson landed on his back and Paloma landed on top of him.

The passengers and crew began to cheer and clap as Patterson eased the young woman onto the deck. He scrambled to his feet and then helped Paloma up.

Paloma gazed at the crew and crowd before lowering her head and covering her eyes. Patterson placed a protective arm around her shoulders as they made their way inside the ship. Doctor Gundervan followed close behind.

"That was horrible," Millie gasped.

"Thank God Patterson was able to reach her in time." Captain Armati shook his head. He turned to Captain Vitale. "We must put her on suicide watch and arrange for her transportation home as soon as we dock in Miami tomorrow."

"Yes sir." Vitale gave a small salute and hurried after Patterson, Paloma and Gundervan.

"I should get back to work," Millie told the captain, who was eyeing the crew still hovering nearby.

"They should too." Captain Armati nodded at Millie and then headed toward the crew, who quickly dispersed when they noticed the captain heading in their direction.

Millie ran into Andy, who was hurrying down the hall. "It's over. Patterson pulled Paloma to safety."

"Whew!" Andy rubbed his brow. "She was going to jump?"

"It sure looked like it. Captain Armati is arranging for her transportation home when the ship docks in Miami tomorrow."

"Many more people leave this ship and there won't be anyone left," Andy joked.

Millie frowned.

"I'm kidding. I was looking for Patterson to see if the lead he was following up on panned out," Andy said. "Do you mind heading backstage to meet with the entertainment staff while I chat with Patterson?"

"Not at all." Millie touched his arm. "I hope he's onto something."

Andy glanced at his watch. "You don't have to meet the crew for another half hour if you want to run up to the lido deck to grab a bite to eat." He pointed at her necklace. "Nice necklace. Did you buy it in St. Thomas?"

Millie lifted her hand and rubbed the tip of her finger over the heart. She smiled. "No. It was a gift."

"Ah." Andy raised a brow. "Glad to hear you and the captain have patched things up." He grinned at Millie and then headed down the steps.

Millie wasn't hungry since she'd just dined with the captain, which was perfect. It would give her enough time to chat with a certain electrician on board.

***

"Paloma...she crazy." Marcus twirled his finger near his temple. "These housekeeping women, I need to stop dating them."

"Do you think Paloma killed Luigi?" Millie asked.

"She crazy in love with him, but then, she was crazy in love with me until she saw bigger fish in the sea, if you know what I mean."

Millie wondered if Marcus knew about Paloma's pregnancy. She had a hunch he did not.

"So you and Paloma dated and then she moved on to Luigi, your boss?

"Yes." Marcus nodded.

"Let's go back to the karaoke area, where we found the power strip. You said it didn't belong to the ship because all of the power strips have the safety trip."

"Yes. That power strip was not ours," Marcus confirmed.

"Where do you think the power strip came from?" Millie asked, and then it dawned on her. "Perhaps it belonged to one of the passengers?"

Marcus scratched his chin thoughtfully. "You think a crewmember stole it from a passenger and then switched it out?"

Millie jumped to her feet. "I think we may be onto something. I'm going down to guest services to see if anyone reported a power strip missing from their cabin."

"I dated a crazed killer." Marcus shook his head.

Millie reached the doorway and turned back. She held a finger to her lips. "You mustn't breathe a word about this, Marcus."

"No Miss Millie. I will not," the man promised. "I gotta start checking these girlfriends' backgrounds before becoming involved."

Millie headed up to the guest services desk and her heart sank when she discovered Nikki Tan was not working. She would have to return later. For now, the show must go on and it was time to head backstage.

She met with the dancers for a brief pre-show meeting and then spent the next hour darting back and forth, helping them switch outfits between performances.

As soon as the show ended, Andy arrived on scene and the two of them worked to put the dancers' costumes, including shoes, accessories and headdresses away.

When they finally took a breather, Millie asked if Andy had any new information.

"No. Patterson talked to Paloma and she swears up and down she had nothing to do with Luigi's death and she's devastated." Andy placed a feathered boa on the hook and shook his head. "The jerk, God rest his soul, told Paloma he planned to divorce his wife and that he was going to marry her."

He went on. "She doesn't seem like the killer-type, not that I've known many killers in my life."

Millie was exhausted. It had been a long day, even though it was only quarter till ten. More than anything she wanted to go back to her cabin, crawl into bed and pretend the countdown for both the captain's departure and Andy's arrest wasn't hours away.

Instead, she grabbed a quick cup of coffee up on the lido deck and then made her way back to guest services.

Millie's friend, Nikki, was working. There was a long line of passengers, waiting to talk to someone in guest services, and the line snaked all the way around the room.

The guest services area was always a zoo the last day of the cruise, and an area Millie avoided if possible. Passengers received copies of their onboard charges the last day of the cruise, and many of them visited guest services to either complain about the charges or try to dispute them.

Millie waited off to the side until there was a lull in the crowd before hurrying over to the desk.

Nikki smiled as Millie approached. "Hello Millie."

"I have no idea how you keep a smile on your face after dealing with all these disgruntled passengers."

"Years of practice," Nikki joked. "What can I do for you?"

"I was wondering if any of the passengers reported a missing power strip during this cruise," Millie said.

"Not that I've heard." Nikki shook her head. "Let me check the system. We keep a detailed log of each passenger's complaint." She shifted her gaze and stared at the computer screen before reaching for the mouse. "As a matter of fact, we did. It was a couple days ago. A passenger by the name of Cathy Dennison reported her power strip had gone missing."

Nikki eyed Millie. "The power strip from the other night, the one that you and the crew found near the karaoke...that was it. You think someone stole a passenger's power strip and hooked it up near the stage in an attempt to electrocute someone."

"Me," Millie said. "I think they were after me." She pointed at the computer. "One more favor. Can you tell me where this passenger's cabin was located?"

"Sure." Nikki reached for the mouse. "Cabin 11202, up on the..."

Millie lifted a hand. I know exactly where that's at. It's the spa suites and where Paloma Herdez works."

Chapter 23

Millie glanced at her watch. The housekeeping staff worked late into the evening for turndown service. She knew Paloma wasn't working and was more than likely sitting inside the medical center where Doctor Gundervan and his staff could keep a close eye on her until they could get her off the ship the following morning for her journey home.

Something was nagging in the back of Millie's mind. When she reached the cabin, she pulled Danielle's cell phone from the desk drawer, switched it on and studied the fuzzy picture of Marcus and Paloma.

There was some small clue she couldn't put her finger on. Perhaps it was because she was exhausted and stressed out.

She reached up and touched the necklace Captain Armati had given her. Maybe a trip up to the spa suites would help jog her memory. She exited the cabin and strode down the hall. As she climbed the stairs, she vowed after this, she was going to bed.

Millie had run out of ideas. There was nothing she could do to clear Andy's name, to keep the captain on board the ship or help poor Paloma.

Millie made a detour to Annette's kitchen to update her on all that had happened since that morning, but the galley was empty so she retraced her steps and headed to deck eleven.

The hall appeared to be empty except for a housekeeping cart shoved against one of the hall walls. She hurried down the hall, making her way past the first cart. There was another cart, farther down the hall and on the same side.

Millie heard someone humming as she passed by the second cart. One of the passenger's suite doors was propped open and inside the suite was a crewmember, bent over the side of the unmade bed.

"Hello?"

The humming stopped. The person stood upright and spun on their heel. "Yes? Can I help you?"

"I was wondering," Millie said as she stepped into the suite. "This spa suite area is small. How many housekeeping staff members cover this section?"

The petite, dark-haired woman stepped closer. She looked vaguely familiar. Millie glanced at the nametag the woman was wearing, *Hazelle*.

Millie's heart skipped a beat as she studied the woman's face. This was it. The clue. Hazelle, Paloma's cabin mate, also worked on this deck. "You're Paloma's cabin mate." It was a statement, not a question.

"I am." The woman's eyes narrowed and she glanced at Millie's tag. "You are the assistant cruise director, the one who broke into our cabin the other morning."

Millie took a step back. "Broke is kind of a strong word. It was more like entered, accessed, not really 'broke.'"

"What do you want?" The woman crossed her arms and leaned forward. She looked a lot like Paloma. Dark hair, dark eyes, olive colored skin. Thin. Petite.

In that instant, the last piece of the puzzle fell into place. The phone in Paloma and Hazelle's cabin belonged to Hazelle. The blurry picture on the phone was *Hazelle* and Marcus. "You dated Marcus, one of the electrical engineers," Millie said as she remembered Marcus' comment about dating crazy women in the housekeeping department.

The woman took a step closer. "No," she said.

Millie pressed on. "You found out Marcus was still chasing after Paloma. I saw the picture of you and Marcus, taken not long ago."

"I..."

Millie cut Hazelle off. "You found out about Paloma and Luigi's secret relationship. Maybe you even knew about the baby and thought it might be Marcus' baby so you decided to kill Luigi and throw Paloma under the bus. She's gone. You get Marcus back."

"But it was your boss, the Cruise Director, Andy Walker. He killed Luigi," Hazelle insisted.

Millie shook her head. "You knew that theory wouldn't hold water and that the secret relationship between Luigi and Paloma would be uncovered and she was the perfect suspect."

"Then, when you found out I had been inside your cabin, you panicked. You realized your phone was in the drawer and there was a good chance I'd seen the picture."

"You worried that when the investigators discovered the relationship between you and Marcus, they might start taking a closer look at you."

She went on. "So you stole one of the passengers' power strips, knowing it was a fire hazard or electrical hazard and you hooked it up to the karaoke stage. Because I was in charge of karaoke, you hoped you would be able to silence me but it backfired."

Hazelle took a menacing step toward Millie, a dark look in her eyes. "You should have kept out of this. Luigi deserved to die. Paloma should've jumped off the ship today after discovering the note Luigi wrote before his death."

"What note?"

"The note where he told her he was ending the relationship and he wanted her to get rid of the baby, that he didn't want it," Hazelle sneered.

A bolt of fear ran down Millie's spine as she stared into the eyes of one of the evilest people she had ever met. "Luigi never wrote a note," Millie said. "You wrote it and convinced your cabin mate, your friend, Paloma, the only way out was to take her own life. Think of the shame, the dishonor Paloma would face, having to return home unwed, with a baby on the way and the baby's father, a married man, dead."

Millie turned to go. "I'm going to tell Dave Patterson what I know." She caught a small movement out of the corner of her eye, right before she felt a crushing pressure on her windpipe. Seconds later, everything went dark.

Chapter 24

Millie's eyes fluttered as she attempted to open them. She tried to lift her head but a dull, throbbing pain caused her to reach for her throat instead.

She heard a shuffling noise and Doctor Gundervan appeared in Millie's line of vision, a concerned expression on his face. "She's coming to," he said.

Millie couldn't see who he was talking to. "What happened?" she croaked.

"Hazelle Kahn tried to strangle you." Millie shifted her gaze to the voice nearby. It was Captain Armati. He reached out and gently grasped her hand. "Thank God you're going to be all right."

Millie nodded and then closed her eyes. It was starting to come back. She had confronted Hazelle, and accused her of killing Luigi Falco and attempting to kill her.

They had argued and Millie had told her she was going to Dave Patterson with the information.

"I remember now," Millie whispered. "Hazelle killed Luigi Falco and tried to murder me." She tried to sit up and realized she was lying on a hospital bed.

Dave Patterson stepped forward. "We've arrested Hazelle for murder and attempted murder. If not for Nikki Tan's concern when she realized you might have been onto Luigi's killer and alerted me, Hazelle may have claimed another victim and gotten away with another murder."

Millie tried to speak, to explain what had happened, but everyone insisted she rest. She was exhausted and, with the knowledge that Andy was now safe, she drifted off to sleep.

When Millie awoke some time later, there was only a small, dull throb in her throat and everyone was gone except for Andy, who was asleep in the chair next to her bed.

She stirred, which woke Andy and he jerked upright.

"What are you doing here?" Millie asked. "You should be in bed."

Andy rubbed his eyes and yawned. "I can't leave my heroine all alone," he teased. "If not for you, I'd be in the brig by now."

"True." Millie smoothed the hospital sheet and grinned. "This ought to be good for something. I've got an idea. How 'bout an early end to my latest probation?"

"Sorry. You'll have to take that up with Patterson." Andy shook his head. "If it were up to me, I'd give you a free pass for the whole year."

"Ah. I see our patient is awake." Doctor Gundervan strolled into the room and placed his hand on the back of Andy's chair. "How are you feeling?"

"Much better." Millie shoved the sheet aside. "I'm ready to blow this Popsicle stand."

"Not so fast." Doctor Gundervan held up a hand. "I want to take a quick peek at you before I cut you loose."

Andy jumped out of his chair. "I'll be out in the front waiting room." He headed to the door, closing it behind him.

Doctor Gundervan checked Millie's pulse, her blood pressure, her temperature, and then turned on his pen light before examining her throat. He finished by inspecting the sides of her neck. "You may have some bruising on your neck but it appears you're no worse for the wear."

"Good." Millie slid off the bed, grateful she was still wearing her clothes and not a hospital gown.

"You can leave on one condition." Doctor Gundervan followed her to the waiting room. "That you stop back sometime later today for a quick check-up."

"Will do." Millie reached for the door handle.

"Maybe now Captain Armati will stop calling down here every fifteen minutes to find out how you're doing," the doctor joked as he opened the door.

Millie turned a tinge of pink and automatically reached for the necklace, which was gone. "My necklace!" she gasped.

"Your necklace is safe and sound," the doctor said. "It's in a small envelope on my desk."

Millie stepped into the waiting room, her eyes automatically scanning the desk. She picked up a white envelope sitting on the side, flipped the flap and reached inside.

Andy sprang out of his chair. "Ready for me to walk you home so you can get a few hours shut eye before turnaround day?"

"More than ready," Millie nodded as she waited for Andy to open the door and they stepped into the hall. She couldn't wait to talk to Patterson, to get his take on Hazelle's arrest.

Chapter 25

Early the next morning, Millie made a beeline for Patterson's office where he shared Hazelle's confession with her.

He told her as soon as the customs' agents gave Siren of the Seas the all clear, the Miami authorities, who were waiting on the dock, would board the ship and escort Hazelle off.

"You'll need to keep your radio on today. The authorities will want a written statement from you," Patterson said.

When the full story unfolded, Hazelle admitted she had dated Marcus after he and Paloma had broken up. After the breakup, Paloma had started dating Luigi Falco. When Hazelle inadvertently discovered Paloma was pregnant, she wasn't certain if the child belonged to Marcus or Luigi; although Paloma had insisted the baby belonged to Luigi.

Hazelle believed if Marcus found out about Paloma's pregnancy, he would dump her and try to get Paloma back, so she hatched a plan to set Paloma up by murdering her boyfriend and making it look as if Paloma had done it.

Although Hazelle knew about Andy's arrest, she figured the charges wouldn't stick and the next person the investigators would turn to would be Paloma. She had convinced Paloma the authorities were close to arresting her and then pointed out in their culture an unmarried pregnant woman was a shame to her family and what was even worse was that the baby's father was a married man.

When the authorities began questioning Hazelle, she ramped up her plan, writing a fake note Luigi had supposedly written to Paloma before his death.

She convinced Paloma the only solution was to commit suicide by jumping off the side of the ship, figuring the authorities would close the investigation after Hazelle told them right before Paloma's death, she'd confessed to her cabin mate and friend that she'd killed Luigi.

It was a foolproof plan until Millie started snooping around. Hazelle panicked, deciding Millie knew too much so she stole a passenger's power strip. She created a fire hazard at the back of the karaoke stage in an attempt to take Millie out.

Patterson continued. "We weren't far behind you in figuring out Hazelle had something to do with Luigi Falco's murder."

"So Paloma never suspected Hazelle of killing Luigi?" Millie asked.

"Nope. She'd pulled the wool over the woman's eyes." Patterson shook his head. "You never know about someone, not even when you live together."

Millie couldn't agree more. She thought about her ex-husband, Roger. "You're right. You can live with someone for years and never really know them."

Patterson eased out of his chair and followed Millie to the door. "There's one more thing. Hazelle confessed to attempting to blackmail an officer of this ship, claiming sexual harassment."

Millie stopped in her tracks. Her blood ran cold. "Captain Armati."

"You didn't hear that from me," Patterson said. "The matter was under preliminary investigation, but now that Hazelle has admitted it wasn't true, the case will be closed."

"So Hazelle tried to blackmail Captain Armati and when it didn't work, she reported he was harassing her."

Patterson nodded. "He wanted to spare the crew having to go through the entire investigation process. Sexual harassment is a very serious charge."

"But now that she's admitted it's not true and has admitted to killing Falco, Captain Armati can remain on board Siren of the Seas."

Patterson shrugged. "It's out of our hands, Millie. Now we'll just have to wait to see what happens."

She glanced at her watch. "I better head upstairs to meet Andy on the gangway. It's time to bid adieu to the passengers. Out with the old and in with the new." Millie wandered out of Patterson's office and strode down the hall.

It was no wonder Captain Armati, Nic, didn't want to tell her the whole reason for his transfer request. She remembered how he'd told her he'd submitted another request, asking to remain on board Siren of the Seas.

If only Captain Armati had trusted her enough to tell her, she would've done whatever she could to help. Maybe he had been trying to protect her.

It was too late now. The captain's...and Millie's, future was in someone else's hands.

***

Millie stood next to Andy on deck five and glanced at the karaoke stage behind them. "You owe me one."

"One what?" Andy smiled. "An extra hour off?" He snapped his fingers. "Tell you what. Remember how much you enjoyed your acupuncture session with Dr. Chow? I'll buy you a month of sessions."

Millie punched her boss in the arm. "That is not funny."

"I could have you swap your karaoke for Danielle's Teen Scene."

"You're kidding," Millie groaned.

"I am." Andy squeezed Millie's arm. "I do owe you one, though. I have a surprise. Meet me in the galley in an hour."

Millie attempted to wheedle the surprise out of Andy but he was tight-lipped and refused to give her a single clue.

After the last passenger had dinged their keycard and exited the ship, Millie ran up to the deli to grab a creamy pesto Panini sandwich the kitchen crew had added to the menu. She carried the sandwich, along with a bag of potato chips, to the corner table.

Cat was there eating her lunch and Millie settled into the seat across from her.

Millie opened the bag of chips and dumped several on the side of her plate. "I haven't seen much of you the last couple of days."

"You've been busy." Cat picked up her piece of cheese pizza and bit the end. "I visited you down in medical after Hazelle took you out, but had to leave before you came to." She pointed to Millie's neck. "She gotcha good."

Millie instinctively reached up and touched the tender spot on the side of her neck. She had attempted to hide the bruises with an extra layer of foundation but there was still a visible spot.

The women chatted about Paloma's unfortunate predicament and Millie said a silent prayer for the young woman. It was a tough spot to be in and she hoped her family would accept her with open arms. She couldn't imagine being alone and pregnant.

Millie changed the subject. "Andy said he has a surprise for me," she said as she picked up her sandwich and nibbled the edge.

"Yep." Cat grinned. "I heard."

"Do you know what it is?"

"Uh-huh, but I've been sworn to secrecy." Cat made a zipping motion across her lips. "You'll find out soon enough."

Cat's demeanor was relaxed and Millie noticed the pinched expression on her face was gone. "How are you doing, Cat? Do you think Dr. Johansen's visit helped?"

"Yes." Cat nodded. "She gave me some great advice about visualizing myself leaving the ship, doing something that made me happy and then visualizing myself returning to the ship. I think it has helped and I'm ready to get off the ship on our next port stop in St. Thomas to prove to myself I can do it."

Cat twirled her straw inside her drink glass. "I visualized you, me and Annette relaxing on a white, sandy beach, soaking up the sun and snorkeling in the crystal clear Caribbean water."

Millie reached for a chip. "Would you like to do that Cat? We can arrange for the day to be a fun one, an island adventure, just the three amigas hanging out."

"You're always busy," Cat said. "So is Annette. I don't want to intrude on your free time."

Millie's heart sank at Cat's words, that she was so busy she didn't have time for her. If she thought about it, the only time she made a point to spend time with her friends was when she needed help during an investigation. "I'm sorry you feel that way, Cat, but it's not true! In fact, we're going to plan our grand adventure. It's high time us girls kicked back and did something fun," Millie vowed.

"I...it would mean a lot to me," Cat simply replied and then glanced at her watch. "We better get going or you'll be late for your surprise."

They hurriedly finished their food and carried their dirty dishes to the bin near the exit. "You're going too?" Millie asked as Cat trailed behind her and they made their way past the deserted pool area to the other side of the ship.

It always struck Millie as odd to see the ship passenger-less, with only the crew on board. It wouldn't be long before the place would be packed with excited vacationers, smiles on their faces, and children racing back and forth across the lido deck.

The ship had recently added small slides and a second splash pool with mushroom-shaped waterfalls. They had even added a toddler zone, now one of the most popular areas on board the ship.

When they reached the stairs on the other side of the pool area, the women descended several flights until they reached deck seven. "Am I going to like my surprise?" Millie asked as she held the door for Cat.

"I hope so," Cat said. When they got close to the galley, Cat hurried ahead and blocked the entrance. "Let me make sure everything is in place. Stay here." She disappeared through the swinging door and emerged moments later. "They're ready for you."

Millie didn't have time to wonder who "they" were as Cat pushed the door open and motioned her friend inside.

Chapter 26

"Surprise!" Loud voices echoed inside the galley.

Annette, Amit, Danielle, Donovan Sweeney, Dave Patterson, Nikki Tan, Felix, Alison, Doctor Gundervan, Andy, and last but not least, Captain Armati stood lined up behind the counter. On top of the counter was a large sheet cake.

Millie's mouth dropped open. "What is this?" It wasn't her birthday, not yet. She made her way over to the counter and stared at the writing on top of the cake, *Congratulations*.

"Congratulations for what?" Millie looked up, a bewildered expression on her face.

"You made it. You finished your first contract," Andy broke from the group and made his way around the counter to stand next to

Millie. "Eight months, Millie. You've been on this ship for eight months."

"No way!" Millie shook her head. "I have?"

"We've put up with you and your snooping for eight long months," Patterson teased.

"Which started on day one," Donovan Sweeney added.

"But we wouldn't have it any other way." Captain Armati said. "You've brought us excitement, adventure..."

"Trouble," Annette quipped.

Laughter erupted and the tips of Millie's ears burned. "Thank you, I think."

Andy cleared his throat and reached into his front pocket, pulling out a sheet of paper. "Without further ado." He unfolded the paper and handed it to Millie. "This is an offer for you to return to Siren of the Seas for another contract, right after your break."

"Break?" Millie shook her head and then it dawned on her. "It's time to go home."

"Yes. It's time to take a break, time to go home and see your family...your other family," Donovan Sweeney said. "Where you can relax and have a little peace and quiet."

"And us, too," Patterson quipped.

Millie took the piece of paper from Andy and stared at the words. "When do I leave? With everything that has gone on, I lost track of time."

"Next week," Captain Armati said softly. "You leave next week."

Which was the exact time Captain Armati was leaving, except he wasn't going on vacation and coming back.

Millie had seven days to pack, to prepare for her trip home, to say good-bye to the love of her life...

"Well?" Annette prompted.

"Well what?" Millie placed the sheet on the counter and gazed at her friend.

"Are you going to come back or have you had enough?"

"You can't get rid of me that easily," Millie said. "I'll be back, so don't even think about replacing me."

Captain Armati placed an arm around Millie's shoulder. "We'll all be back on board Siren of the Seas, one way or another."

The end.

The series continues. Look for book #8, coming soon...

If you enjoyed reading "Killer Karaoke", please take a moment to leave a review. It would be greatly appreciated! Thank you!

Meet The Author

Hope Callaghan is an author who loves to write Christian books, especially Christian Mystery and Cozy Mystery books. She has written more than 45 mystery books (and counting) in five series.

Born and raised in a small town in West Michigan, she now lives in Florida with her husband.

She is the proud mother of one daughter and a stepdaughter and stepson. When she's not doing the thing she loves best - writing books - she enjoys cooking, traveling and reading books.

Hope loves to connect with her readers! Connect with her today!

Visit **hopecallaghan.com** for special offers, free books, and soon-to-be-released books!

Email: hope@hopecallaghan.com

Facebook:
https://www.facebook.com/hopecallaghanauthor/

Creamy Pesto Panini Sandwich Recipe

Ingredients:

For the Creamy Pesto:
1 cup fresh basil, packed
2 tablespoons olive oil
1/2 cup chopped walnuts
2 cloves garlic
1/2 cup parmesan cheese
1/2 teaspoon salt
1/4 teaspoon pepper
1 tablespoon lemon juice
4 ounces cream cheese (whipped works best)

For the Panini Sandwich Recipe:
8 slices sour dough bread
Softened butter
16 slices thinly sliced smoked turkey
12 slices cooked bacon
1 cup shredded mozzarella cheese
1 can artichoke hearts, drained and pulled apart
(optional)

Directions:

-Preheat a Panini press to 300 degrees F. Add the ingredients for the creamy pesto to a food processor. Puree until smooth.

-Butter one side of the slices of bread. Flip them over and spread the creamy pesto on the opposite side.

-Place 4 slices, butter side down, on the Panini press. Layer each slice (the side with the creamy pesto) with a small handful of artichokes leaves, 4 pieces of smoked turkey, 3 slices of bacon, and a handful of mozzarella cheese. Place the other slice of bread on top, butter side up.

-Close the Panini press and grill for 3-5 minutes.

-Serve warm.

*4 Servings

(You could also substitute a few green olives for the salt.)

Made in the USA
Middletown, DE
25 September 2023